DIVIDED BY BLOOD

DIVIDED BY BLOOD

a novel by
Rebekah S. Cole

This book is a work of fiction. Names, characters, businesses, organizations, places, events and incidents either are the product of the author's imagination or are used fictitiously. Any resemblance to actual persons, living or dead, events, or locales is entirely coincidental.

For information about special discounts for bulk purchases or to book an event, please contact SimchahScripts@gmail.com.

Graphic Design by Mario Patterson

Published and Printed in the United States of America.

First Edition
ISBN 9781790434091

CreateSpace Independent Publishing Platform
North Charleston, SC

DEDICATION

To those who understand that you can pick your nose, but not your family...

DIVIDED BY BLOOD

Prologue

The day of the funeral was grey and humid. It was threatening to rain all morning and Jonetta wished the sky would open up to pour down on them. Her spirit was broken and she wanted to walk barefoot in the woods while it rained just as she used to do back in Pennsylvania. She did not utter a word to anyone about what she knew. The truth was too unbearable. Unthinkable. Instead, her piercing eyes were locked on the casket. *My sister. I'm so sorry.*

The doctor's voice rang in her ears repeatedly, "Her heart simply gave out. It happens to elderly people all the time." However, Jonetta knew better. Other than grief over her beloved Fred, Georgia was healthy and nowhere near death. All the drama that her daughters had brewing lately didn't amount to much since Georgia died.

For just a moment, they all pushed their petty issues aside to come together as a family. Phyllis sobered up quickly once her secret was aired on social media. The news of their only aunt in Chicago dying made her grow closer to Damien. Instead of turning up the bottle, she turned to him for comfort and in return, he welcomed this tender, vulnerable side of her. They sat inside the funeral home with the twins holding one another. Damien softly kissed her forehead as she placed her head on his shoulder.

Colette finally broke from her cloud of delusion and apologized to her mother once she learned that Georgia died. She packed her things at the church in silence as the women asked her questions about Pastor's condition and her reasons for leaving, but she remained silent. *You'll find out soon enough!* Now that she had the house to herself with her children, she quickly realized how much of a help Georgia had been to her ever since she moved in after the fire. Since her relationship with her mother was strained, she couldn't look to her for help. Regardless of her anger towards Pastor, she was still going to use his attorney to finalize her divorce with Owen. She needed to get those papers signed and filed while Pastor was still in the hospital. Moving forward was her mission at this point and nobody was going to stop her.

Jonetta inhaled deeply, closed her eyes and allowed a single tear to trickle down her face. She once believed that her daughters were going to give her a heart attack, but as grief took over these past few days, she was convinced that sadness and regret could do the job even better. A tight knot formed in her throat as turmoil erupted in the pit of her stomach. She covered her mouth to keep from making any sound that resembled a gag.

Phyllis grabbed her mother's hand and whispered, "Are you alright?"

Jonetta nodded and squeezed her daughter's hand in return. She was a sweetheart when she wanted to be one.

"Has anybody seen Dawn?" Jonetta asked.

"Not yet, Mama," Colette replied, leaning forward. "You know she's always running behind unless it's for one of her gigs."

"I sent her a text, but she hasn't responded yet." Phyllis said.

"Where did she sleep last night? At Chena's house or Shon's?"

"Who is Shon?" Phyllis asked.

"Her new guy, my old boss, Doctor Bishon Franklyn." Jonetta responded looking at Phyllis puzzled. "You don't know about him?"

Phyllis cocked her head to the side as she recalled that odd name. *That's the guy who stopped by the house that day.* "Wait a minute…the dentist? Dawn is dating him?"

Jonetta sighed and nodded. *Unfortunately.*

"Mama, I totally forgot, but Aunt Georgia wanted me to tell you something…"

"I have to use the bathroom, mommy!" Serena announced, interrupting Phyllis.

"Shhh…" Phyllis put her finger up to her mouth. "Just a minute."

"Take her to the restroom, Phyllis." Jonetta said softly. "We'll talk later."

The funeral services began and ended so quickly you would think Georgia did not have a full life, but she did. Georgia had been their angel in disguise. She offered herself willingly, selflessly to make sure that her daughters had a place to go for peace. Lately, she had been more of a mother to them than Jonetta. Her heart was pure, free from anger, bitterness and malice. Jonetta never did understand how her sister was so quick to forgive people. She shook her head in awe. *Georgia was something else.* The repast was at Norman's house in a few hours, but she was not in the mood for people. Jonetta sat for a moment in silence as the room cleared out. She looked down at her aging hands, clasped them together, and prayed for forgiveness.

"Owen is here," Norman alerted Colette in the foyer. "But please don't cause a scene today. Your mother is too fragile right now for any drama, Colette."

Colette nodded. "I just want a divorce, Daddy. Not a fight."

"Divorce isn't that simple," Norman admitted. "I should know…I've gone through it twice."

"Twice?"

"Yeah, I was married before I met your mother."

"That's news to me!"

Norman shrugged and shook his head. "There's so much that you girls just don't know."

"Can we continue this conversation later, Daddy? I really need to talk to Owen."

"Sure, and I need to find your mother."

Jonetta headed to the car to smoke a cigarette. Her nerves were bad and the guilt consumed her. *My hatred for Big Louie killed my own sister! God, what have I done?* She sniffed, flicked a tear away, and stopped in her tracks when she heard a familiar voice.

"Mrs. Miller!" Bishon called from the parking lot. He maneuvered between cars until he reached her.

"Bishon? What are you doing here?" Jonetta asked, confused. "You didn't have to come to the funeral…"

Bishon bowed his head, and slowly looked up to meet her eyes. She could tell that he had been crying and found it very odd. *He didn't even know Georgia.*

"Where's Dawn?" Jonetta asked. "Did she ride with you here?"

"No, I haven't seen Dawn."

That's odd. Where the hell is Dawn? "Well, what's wrong, Bishon?"

"I finally found my mother," he said just above a whisper.

"That's good news!" Jonetta replied, touching his shoulder. "I needed to hear some good news today. How did you find her?"

"Turns out that my Dad knew more than he wanted to admit. He finally told me that he knew the woman who dropped me off at the church, but she wasn't the mother. It was her niece's baby. She had told my Dad that her niece was too young to raise a baby and… they had a business to run… so…she told her that the baby died."

Dawn sat in the car as she nervously watched Bishon and her mother talking. "Mama, what are you doing? Please don't tell him I'm pregnant." She glanced in the rear view mirror to check her eyes. They were still red. *Shit! I hope that Mama will just think I've been crying so I wont' have to tell her that I was almost choked to death!* She placed her dark sunglasses on and fixed the scarf around her neck before she exited the car.

"That's terrible. Is your mother still alive?" Jonetta asked.

"Very much so," he replied nodding his head.

"Oh, good! Who is she? Where is she?" Jonetta asked anxiously.

"My birth mother lived in a brothel ran by her two aunts in Beverly. She was a prostitute...back then. My mother thought her baby was stillborn."

Bishon stared at Jonetta without uttering another word. His eyes welled with tears that were threatening to stream down his face. Jonetta raised her eyebrows as she realized what he had just explained. Suddenly, her expression drastically changed from expecting an answer to knowing the answer. Her mouth slowly dropped open as she clutched her necklace taking deep quick breaths. Jonetta tried to form a sentence as her bottom lip quivered, but only more quickened breaths escaped. *Oh, my God!*

All these years Jonetta had believed that her Aunt Betty Lou had tossed her stillborn son in the trash, like she admitted on her deathbed. Jonetta hated her aunt for it, almost smothered her to death over it! Jonetta inhaled sharply as her whole body trembled as she realized what this meant to her and her daughters. *I have a son? My girls have a brother?* Her eyes widened as she thought about the news Dawn had recently shared with her. *Dawn is pregnant by...*

"Oh, my God! Dawn!"

Bishon nodded and sobbed. "I didn't know that she was my sister..."

Jonetta clutched her chest, then reached for Bishon's shoulder but missed making contact by inches. Bishon caught her before she hit the ground.

"Mama!" Dawn screamed, rushing towards them. "Somebody call an ambulance!"

Chapter 1

"*When I wake up from this nightmare, I'm going to wrap my arms around him. All this time, all these years, I thought he was dead. There he was right in front of my face! I'm wasting more time lying here. God, I know that I have a lot of nerve talking to you after what I've just done to my own sister, but... but that was an accident. You know that! I know you see me and hear me. Get me out of this hospital! I want to wake up and talk to him! There's way too many unanswered questions.*

The sound of voices and feet shuffling stifled her prayers momentarily.

Dear God, what about Dawn? Oh, God, what a disaster! Does she know by now? Do any of my daughters even know by now? Just let me open my eyes so I can see what's going on out there? I can't see a damn thing, Goddammit! Woops! Forgive me, God, for cursing. Just wake me up! Please. I promise that I'll be a better person, a better mother, if you wake me up from this nightmare. Hell, I might even go to church."

"Mr. Miller, you can see your wife now." A deep voice said and grew closer.

"*Wife? We're divorced, thank you very much!"*

"Thank you, doc. What happened?" Norman cleared his throat waiting to hear Jonetta's diagnosis.

"I'm doctor McCullough," he extended his hand to greet Norman. "Mrs. Miller suffered from a mild stroke. By tomorrow morning, she'll be groggy and by afternoon she should be able to communicate. We have her sedated for now so her body can rest."

"What? Who asked you to do that? Unplug the drugs right this minute!"

"It'll be fine by me if she can't talk for a while." Normal chuckled to himself.

"Bastard!"

The deep voice continued, "At her age, we can never be too sure about recovery. We really won't know the extent until all the test results are back. Then we can determine if physical therapy or any prescriptions will be needed."

"When will the results be ready?"

"In a couple of hours, at the very latest, early morning." The doctor held the electronic chart pad to his chest and rested his hand on Norman's shoulder. "Listen, your wife is under great care right now. However, going forward her stress level must be at a minimum. We want a full recovery, right?"

Norman nodded, "Doctor's orders." He shook his hand firmly and sighed. "Thanks doc."

"The nurse will be right in, feel free to have a seat next to the bed."

"Oh, uhhh… doc… I have my daughters, grandkids and a few friends waiting in the lobby. Can they come in to visit?"

"Friends? What damn friends? Must be yours! I only want to see my children…all of them!"

"You'll have to discuss that with the nurse. Good luck," he responded and left the room quickly.

Norman grunted as he pulled a chair by Jonetta's bedside. He sat down heavily, gazing at all the whizzing machines, beeping monitors, and long tubes dangling from each machine. "Oh, my Netta, my Netta. So much going on with our girls and their issues, then your sister dies out of nowhere. It's been rough on you lately, huh?"

"Ya think? I need a cigarette."

Norman squeezed her left hand and if Jonetta could squeeze it back, she would have. Although they were divorced, they lived peaceably together under one roof. Norman had finally earned a place in her bed and wanted to spend more nights in the same bed, but he knew that would take time, especially now.

The combination of the cold room and his emotions caused his nose to drip. He sniffled several times before releasing a sob.

"What on earth? Are you crying?"

Norman heaved and wiped his nose with the back of his hand. "Where's the damn tissue around this place?"

"Oh, my God! He is crying! I'm not dying, you fool! Toughen up!"

"I need you, Netta. You've always been the strong one between us. I don't know how to handle our daughters *and* take care of you. Please get better, Netta. God, help me."

A young nurse entered the room interrupting Norman's confession. He quickly wiped his face free of tears that streamed down his face.

"Hello, I'm nurse Trulie and I'll be taking care of your wife tonight." She introduced herself with a Southern drawl as she swiped a loose red curl from her face, placing it behind her ear and plastered a polite smile.

"For the love of God, I'm not his wife... Nevermind. Nobody can hear me anyway."

"Trulie?"

The nurse chuckled, "Yes, like the word truly but spelled like Julie." She pointed to her nametag and continued explaining Jonetta's vitals. It all went over his head and she was talking way too fast for him to even grasp a full understanding.

"Look, ummmm... I hate to interrupt you, but your accent let's me know you're not from Chicago. So, it would be helpful if my daughters were in here to listen to all of this too. I may forget something along the way or not understand your medical lingo."

"I understand, Mr. Miller, my Kentucky drawl throws a lot of people off. As far as visitors, only two other people can come into the room at this time. The others will have to wait until morning," she explained the hospital policy with a toothy grin. "Why don't you bring whomever you like in here now before I see about my next patient?"

Chapter 2

"What happened?" Colette asked frantically, entering the Emergency Room lobby with her three children in tow and Delilah on her hip. She looked to her sisters for answers, as the rest of the faces were unfamiliar.

"I… I don't know…" Dawn replied in a strained tone, adjusting her black shades. "I had just got there in the parking lot … and … that's when I saw Mama talking to Bishon and then she hit the ground."

Bishon shifted nervously, nodded and cleared his throat prepared to explain, but was cut off before he had the chance.

"Where were you anyway? You missed the whole funeral!" Phyllis hissed at Dawn. "Nevermind, this is a nightmare!" Phyllis replied in angst, waving her hand. "One minute we're saying our goodbyes to Aunt Georgia, the next minute we're rushing Mama to the hospital." Damien caressed her shoulders, being the loving husband he had always been, she welcomed his touch and buried her face in his chest.

"Well, what are the doctors saying? Did Mama have a heatstroke? Was Aunt Georgia's death just too much for her? What is going on?" Colette rambled off possibilities without taking a breath. "Cornell, go sit with your cousins." She motioned for the children to take seats in a corner where their cousins, Sabrina and Serena, were sitting quietly distracted by the television. Delilah squirmed on her hip, clearly frustrating Colette.

"I'll take her," Dawn offered. Delilah was reluctant to release her mother, clutching onto her blouse, but Dawn won that battle. "Come to aunty, baby. I got you." She continued talking to her in a singsong voice right when Delilah snatched the sunglasses from her face. Dawn gasped and quickly turned her back from her family so they wouldn't see her bloodshot eyes. She successfully plucked her sunglasses from Delilah's tight grip and placed them back on her face. *You're going back to your Mama in two seconds little girl!*

Bishon touched her elbow gently, "Are you alright?"

Dawn tensed at his touch. "Yeah, I'm good."

"Can we talk?" Bishon whispered. Dawn grew concerned by the worry etched in his face.

"Grandpa!" Serena yelled and bolted across the room to wrap around his legs. Sabrina followed and held onto the other side of him.

"Dad, what's going on with Mama?" Colette rushed towards him and Dawn followed.

Saved by my Dad! Thank God! Dawn thought as she joined her family.

"Listen up everyone," Norman raised his hands in the air, commanding attention from everyone in ear shot. "Your mom has suffered a mild stroke."

Groans and gasps filled the air.

"When can we see her?" Colette asked anxiously. Her young daughters, Lydia and Ruthie, crowded around her silently. Cornell did not budge from the television; he had become immune to drama in his family.

"Your mom is heavily sedated right now. The nurse told me only two of you can come back right now and the rest can come back tomorrow during visiting hours."

"What? We all want to see Mama!" Dawn replied almost whining, shifting Delilah on her bony hip.

"Well, since I'm the oldest, I'm definitely going back." Phyllis said, grabbing her purse from the chair in the lobby.

"Is that how this is gonna work?" Dawn retorted. "I get the short end of the stick because I'm the youngest? Be for real! I wanna see my Mama, too!"

"We heard you the first time, but I agree with Phyllis on this one." Colette chimed in already headed towards the double doors. "You and the fellas can keep an eye on the kids while we're back there. Cornell can help out too. Right?"

A disagreement ensued amongst the adults and the children began to nit-pick at one another.

"Figure it out! I'll be in room one thirty-two with your Mama when you're ready." Norman stormed off, fed up with his daughters' behavior.

***

"Who is that crying?"

"When will she wake up?" Colette asked resting her hand on her mother's knee.

"The doctor said by tomorrow afternoon," Norman replied hopeful. "We'll be able to talk to her and get down to the bottom of all of this. I think the funeral was just too much especially with everything going on." Norman wrapped his arms around Colette and Phyllis, pulling them closer to him. He planted a quick kiss on their cheeks for reassurance.

Phyllis abruptly pulled away from her father's hold. "Mama, it's Phyllis. I don't know what that man said to you nor why he's even here, but if he did something to you, so help me God…"

"What man?" Norman asked confused.

"That doctor. Mama's former boss. He's supposedly dating Dawn or something," Phyllis explained concisely as possible. "I don't like him. He came to the house and everything!"

"When did he come to our house?" Colette asked, confused just like Norman.

"That's what I'd like to know too!"

"Bishon? Dr. Franklyn?"

"Yeah! That's his weird name." Phyllis snapped her fingers. "I don't like him one bit."

Norman waved her off. "Oh, he's harmless."

"How would you know, Dad?"

"Norman! Don't say another word!"

"He's my friend's son. You know my friend and his wife, Stanton and Barbara."

Phyllis cocked her head to the side.

"Listen, we'll talk about it later, baby." Norman placed a hand on his daughter's shoulder to ease her concern. "The doctor said your mother needs rest, no stress, and she may need therapy."

"Thank you! Yes, get them focused back on me."

"Therapy?" Colette placed her hand over her mouth.

"Yes, Colette." Phyllis rolled her eyes. "That's usually needed after someone has a stroke."

"You don't have to be such a smart ass all the time!"

"You don't have to always be a damn blonde!"

"Girls! Stop it! Do you not see me lying in a hospital bed? For God's sake!"

"Girls!" Norman strained sternly. "Do you wanna get kicked out of your own Mama's hospital room? Pull yourselves together!"

"Where's my baby? Somebody had better go get Dawn. Lord, all I need is for Bishon to go telling Dawn what she's not prepared to even hear. Not now. Not without her Mama by her side."

"Mama, we're going to get you out of here soon," Phyllis said squeezing her hand.

Chapter 3

A wave of grief swept over her as she pulled up to the curbside and thought about what took place with her mother at the cemetery, not being able to see Jonetta at the hospital and now whatever drama was waiting for her on the other side of the door. It was all weighing heavily on her spirit. Dawn searched the glove compartment for a joint, but quickly slammed it shut as she reminded herself that she literally had a life or death decision to make before she indulged. Instead, she practiced her breathing exercises that she learned from yoga. The humming from the engine matched her soft humming. The brief serenity didn't wipe away her feeling of dread.

Dawn knew once she entered that house Colette would try to make her feel guilty about leaving her and the kids at a time like this, but her mind was made up. She could manage the pathetic attempts her sister would toss her way to convince her to stay in that house with her, but not the tender hugs from her nieces and nephew when she told them good-bye. *Those are her kids, not mine. I have enough to worry about.*

God give me the strength. She shuddered as she turned off the ignition to the Mercedes E550 that her Aunt Georgia left behind. Gabe and Georgia took such great care of everything that they owned. The Mercedes, although 10 years old was still in mint condition. Even the leather seats were like brand new. Her aunt and uncle certainly enjoyed the finer things in life. Gabe was able to provide it for her since he owned several businesses that Georgia liquidated after he died a year ago. Since her death, nobody had mentioned a will just yet, so Dawn took it upon herself to claim the car as her own. Naturally. She was the only one driving it while Georgia was alive anyway. Besides, it was moot point to even discuss rightful ownership of the car because Colette didn't even have a driver's license. She could call for an Uber driver if she really needed to get somewhere, Dawn figured.

Getting hold of a will was a whole other beast that the family would need to figure out soon because Georgia was sitting on a chunk of change. It was far from everyone's mind since Jonetta was in the hospital. But once the medical bills start piling up it was going to be on the tip of her tongue, if not sooner.

"Now is not the time to just bail on me and the kids!" Colette said frantically.

"I'm not 'bailing' on you!" Dawn objected. "Trust me, girl, this is not about you or the kids… I just… Listen, just trust me, this is for the best for both of us. Trust me."

"How is moving in with Phyllis better than living here with me? She has kids at her house, too!"

Dawn shook her head. *This girl is always in competition with somebody.* A notification popped up on her phone. It was a text from Raffi. She swiped it away. *I don't have time for you right now.*

"This isn't about who has the most kids. Please believe me!" Dawn replied, tossing toiletries in her Gucci Techno bag.

"Were you *not* in the hospital last night? We don't even know if Mama will recover fully from this stroke. Aunt Georgia… just … up and died on me. Owen is with that whore expecting another baby. And now… you want to leave me, too?"

Dawn ran her fingers through her curly locks, clenching her eyes as she exhaled. When she opened her eyes she focused on the Gucci bag and knots grew in her stomach. Her thoughts traveled back to how she got the bag in her possession in the first place. The fashion industry was not built for those faint at heart. Sometimes, she missed that fast life. It was a rush being on the runway, being dolled up with exotic hair and make-up, wearing couture fashion and having the crowd rave for more. But once she was off the runway, the other part of fashion reared its ugly head.

There were lots of ugly, uncircumcised heads and venomous souls in the industry. Some men and women she had the pleasure of rejecting, others she felt there was no other choice but to satisfy them with whatever they wanted from her.

Now that Dawn was finally taking control of her life, it was her sister who was trying to manipulate her this time. No. She couldn't allow it.

"I love you and the kids, girl," she managed to say after shoving back the memories of her former life. "It's too much sadness in this house. I just need a change of scenery and energy."

This time her cell phone rang breaking the tension in the air. *Whew! Thank God!* Dawn thought as she searched her purse for her phone. Immediately, she frowned, but answered anyway. She motioned to her sister that she was going to take the call in another room.

"Hello," Dawn answered, closing the first floor bathroom door behind her.

"You left the hospital without talking to me," Bishon said with a slight desperation in his voice.

Dude, for real? Keeping her yoga practices in mind, Dawn inhaled sharply before replying and exhaled slowly. "There was a lot going on with my family. I was completely frustrated that I didn't get a chance to even see my mother," Dawn explained. "I appreciate your concern for my mom, but please don't feel obligated to show up."

"Well, actually, that's what I wanted to talk to you about. Do you think we can meet today?"

"No. Today isn't good at all."

"What about tomorrow?"

Dawn sighed, growing frustrated with his persistence. At this point, her goal was pack her things, move in with Phyllis and go see her Mama. The last thing she wanted to do was be in Bishon's company. Would she even be able to look him in the eye at this point?

"Dawn?" Bishon interrupted her thoughts.

"You want to discuss my mother with me? I'm confused," Dawn became flustered, worried that she was about to lose her patience with him. "Is it something about when she worked for your dental office? Do you need me to complete some paperwork for her?"

"No, it's nothing like that," Bishon chuckled nervously. "I'll explain more when I see you… hopefully, tomorrow."

"Honestly, I'm in the middle of moving and I'm a bit overwhelmed with everything as you can imagine," Dawn tried to explain so he could get the hint.

"You're moving? Where to? Hopefully, not back to New York."

Damn! Nosey are we? "No. I'm just bouncing from one sister to the other. I really can't get into a discussion about it now. So, just let me get back to you some time tomorrow."

"The sooner, the better," Bishon added for good measure, hoping Dawn would get the hint of urgency.

"I'll know better tomorrow *after* I see my mother." Dawn's voice trailed off as she thought about her mother lying there incoherent in a cold, sterile hospital. "I'll call you tomorrow to confirm."

Bishon let out a sigh of relief. "I'll see you soon." Dawn ended the call without saying goodbye.

Chapter 4

The moment Dr. Bishon Franklyn hung up the phone, he began grinding his teeth. A nasty habit that he picked up while studying for dental exams. Of course, he knew better being a dentist, but when his nerves got the better of him instantly he would grind unconsciously. This time he was grinding his teeth due to being frustrated that he had not successfully spoken to Dawn since Jonetta passed out in the parking lot. All things considered, he was lucky at this point that nobody had questioned what he was discussing with Jonetta. They were all focused on her recovery, rightfully so, as was he.

Had he used more wisdom, none of this would've ever happened. But he had been so anxious to share his news with Jonetta that he selfishly tracked her down and spilled his guts. He clenched his eyes tight and rubbed his forehead silently beating himself up for not keeping his mouth shut. *Now look at the mess you've made.*

Over the past 48 hours, his life had been a bulldozer knocking down anything in its path. Normally, Bishon had his affairs in order. He had his own dental practice and slated to open another office on the north side by the end of the year. Although he was nearing fifty-years-old, at six foot two with chestnut eyes, smooth dark skin, fit body and perfect teeth, of course, he rarely had any issues dating. He just had not found anyone compatible until he met Dawn.

The fire and passion in her eyes compelled him to leap before he looked. As a dentist it was necessary to be cautious. Even in his personal life he was cautious and mostly practical, except when it came to Dawn. He had to admit that he was spellbound from the moment she entered his office. Her wild curly hair matched her free spirit. The scent of body oils that floated from her supple skin right up his nose had him wide open and wanting to know more about her.

Most women that he encountered could barely measure up to Dawn and all had the nerve to insist on a 90-day rule when they could barely make it past 30-days without wanting to sleep with him. A young woman as beautiful and successful in the fashion industry as Dawn was, he just knew that she would play hard to get like most of the women he dated. But his pursuit with Dawn was not challenging as he assumed it would. She was carefree and didn't care what other people thought of her and in return she wasn't judgmental of others. She was refreshing. Yes, Dawn was a tease, but that didn't make her easy. She was anything but coy and it only made him hungrier for her.

When he had given her a ride to the airport she opened her legs wide and welcomed his touch. Bishon knew that she was giving him a treat as a promise to give him more. That was the day that he knew he would make love to her sooner than later.

Bishon couldn't wait for her to return from Atlanta. While she was away, her face appeared to him on several occasions, especially at night. Just the very vision of her made his nature rise. When she returned disappointed that her audition for *The Mistresses of Atlanta* didn't go well, he had a special night planned for her. Secretly, he was glad that her audition tanked because that meant she would not be leaving Chicago anytime soon. A distraction is what she needed and he gave it to her, repeatedly all night.

Now he wished that he could hold her, comfort and feel her warmth again, but that would be completely out of the question now. He groaned at the thought of never making love to Dawn again. It was sheer punishment and anguish. Now that it was unnatural to desire her, how would he manage to suppress his feelings for her? What a cruel joke!

Bishon needed comforting, too, ever since he discovered the truth about Jonetta. Everything happened so fast. One minute he was driving to the funeral home, the next minute he was telling Jonetta that she was his mother and the next thing he knew, she was on the ground and sirens were blaring. The guilt riddled through his soul and he needed someone to tell him that everything would be alright. That his birth mother would pull through and she would welcome him in her life for good.

It was Dawn who encouraged him to find his birth mother. Bishon had only toyed with the idea from time-to-time, but a little pillow talk with Dawn convinced him to find his birth mother.

"Regardless if you ever get to meet her, it'll be a freeing experience," she had said one night as he rested across her soft breasts.

It was in that moment that Bishon knew that he needed a woman like Dawn in his life. She was tender when he needed her to be and fierce at the appropriate times. Now, all hopes of ever marrying her and having a few babies with her were all thrown out the window. Bishon grimaced and rubbed his temples. As a rule, he had always told his patients to have candid conversation with him about what pained them so he could treat them properly. Now it was his turn to be candid with everyone.

The only mother and father that he had ever known, Barbara and Stanton Franklyn, wasn't aware that he had discovered the truth about his birth mother. Given the friendship that his father had with Norman Miller, this was going to be such a sensitive subject to broach. Although he was delighted to find his birth mother, it really bothered him that she was right there in front of their faces the whole time.

Bishon exhaled fiercely as he dialed his father's mobile phone. He finally answered on the third ring.

"Hey, Dad. I've got some news to share with you and Mom. I need to swing by as soon as possible."

Chapter 5

The sun made an appearance through the striped forest green curtains. Phyllis meant to pull them tightly closed as she had done every night, but after helping Dawn settle in, she was exhausted and collapsed on the bed. Now the sunlight began to fill the room as each minute passed. It was useless trying to fall back to sleep. She could tell by Damien's breathing that he was slightly awake. Phyllis reached for Damien. He grunted and rolled over.

Years ago, she had learned a hard lesson that she would never forget about trying to convince a man to have sex with her. As a result, once she felt rejection from her husband, all bets were off even if he had a change of heart later. What she had to offer was good, damn good. He knew it, too. That's how she was able to snatch him from his other woman. Phyllis blew his mind in bed. But if he didn't want it, his loss.

Fresh coffee floated through the air straight up her nostrils. Phyllis knew that Dawn was awake and decided to join her sister since there wasn't going to be any action in her bedroom. She peeled the covers off her and plopped them on top of Damien's back. He hated it when she did that and she knew it.

"Good Morning," Phyllis said entering the kitchen. "Coffee smells good. Damien and I really don't make coffee anymore."

"Oh, I made huge pot," Dawn grimaced.

"That's okay, trust me, it will be put to good use." Phyllis smiled. "I saw a great idea on Pinterest for leftover coffee."

Dawn slurped on the hot coffee and nodded her head in approval of the taste.

"All you have to do is pour the leftover coffee into an ice cube tray and the next morning, you have… Iced coffee!" Phyllis clasped her hands together with a huge smile.

Dawn giggled. "You're right, that is a good idea. A method often used at coffee shops for their iced coffees, too."

Phyllis furrowed her brows, and then a few seconds later raised them.

"Vine!" They said simultaneously and shared a laugh.

Dawn winked at her sister and took a small sip from the mug.

Phyllis peered into her sister's mug. "What are you using as creamer?"

"Almond milk and a dash of nutmeg."

Phyllis nodded and followed suit.

"I'm really scared right now," Dawn admitted, placing her mug on the counter.

Phyllis slowly poured Almond milk into her mug before she responded, "Scared of what?"

"All of this uncertainty. I mean… Mama is laid up in the hospital. I wasn't even there when everything went down. Nobody knows what happened to my Mama. Dad is all alone at the house. I just packed up and left Colette all alone with her kids." Dawn shot Phyllis a look. "Colette."

Phyllis shot the knowing look right back and nodded. "Yeah, you did."

Dawn leaned against the counter and shook her head. "I can really be a selfish bitch sometimes. But I just couldn't stay there anymore. Aunt Georgia died in that house and I swear that I can smell her presence." Dawn waved her hand at her last comment. "I know y'all don't believe in spirits like I do, but I swear I can sense her presence in that house."

"Don't beat yourself up so bad," Phyllis replied, pulling out two chairs from the kitchen table. "Sit with me before the little two terrors wake up."

Dawn grabbed her mug and sat at the table. "Believe me, they are angels compared to Colette's kids!"

"You're welcome here, sis. Things won't be easy for any of us for a while. We have to develop a plan to rotate with visiting the hospital and checking up on Dad. Even though he puts on a tough act, I know he's hurting. We have to make sure that he's eating, staying busy, being occupied and not just sulking without Mama."

Dawn nodded. "I have a lot to consider in the meantime."

Phyllis looked puzzled. "How so? You have a roof over your head. You're rolling nice in Aunt Georgia's Mercedes. You have men practically fighting over you. What could be so wrong?"

"I'm pregnant." Dawn confessed.

"Holy shit!" Phyllis covered her mouth. She sprung to her feet to hug her baby sister. "Congratulations, baby sis! Welcome to the mommy-hood club."

Dawn closed her eyes and shook her head. "Not so fast. It's complicated."

With her chin resting on her fist, Dawn explained her complicated situation with Raffi and Chena, the reason she wasn't at the funeral, and her reluctance for sharing the news with Bishon.

"It's okay, sis," Phyllis reassured Dawn with a weak smile. "We'll figure this out. First of all, if your eyes don't clear up by the end of the week, you'll have to see a doctor, for sure. Secondly, Raffi needs his ass beat!" Phyllis sucked her teeth and continued on a softer note, "Whatever you want to do about the baby, remember it's *your* choice. It's *your* body. Don't let anyone make you feel guilty one way or the other. It's going to be okay, I promise."

They embraced and after a moment passed, Phyllis planted a kiss on her baby sister's forehead.

"Wait. Does Mama know about this?"

Dawn nodded and squeezed her sister's hand. Even though she knew everything was far from being okay, she believed it in that moment. Much like Phyllis, she would probably venture down the path of having an abortion. The way things were slowly progressing with Jonetta, she'd have to do it without her mother.

"Are you sure you don't want to ride with me to the hospital to see Mama? I could use the company." Phyllis searched her sister's face, hoping she would agree.

Dawn shook her head no, slowly. "I'll watch the kids and give Damien a break. They don't need to be at the hospital seeing Mama like that." She mindlessly twisted the silver ring engraved with half-moons on her index finger in a circular motion. Dawn wanted her one-on-one time with her mother. She had so much to tell her and wanted to accomplish that privately.

"Well, if that's the case then Damien is going to wake his lazy ass up and ride with me!" Phyllis headed up the stairs. "I need some type of moral support!"

An hour later, the twins were up eating cereal and Damien and Phyllis were out the door.

"We should take full advantage of my sister living with us, ya know?"

"What are you talking about?" Damien asked adjusting the temperature in their SUV.

"We have an in-house babysitter!" Phyllis slapped his arm, laughing.

Damien sucked his teeth. "Dawn can't sit still for a minute. I'll be surprised if she's still in Chicago six months from now. She's totally unreliable."

Phyllis jerked her neck and rolled her eyes. Although, she really couldn't argue with him on that claim, she still didn't want him throwing shade at her sister. "Well, before she leaves us, the least we can do is go on a date for a change."

A song blared across the radio that Phyllis had not heard before, but it was clear that Damien knew it well. Driving in a truck all day afforded him the freedom to tune into radio stations while tuning out the world. He turned up the volume and began to sing along.

"Maybe karaoke night?" she suggested, searching his face.

Damien kept singing.

Phyllis seethed.

As they exited the hospital elevator, Damien slipped his hand inside of hers and squeezed it gently. He knew that he had pissed her off during the car ride by ignoring her discussion of going on a date, but now was not the time for negative energy. Phyllis exhaled and squeezed back, letting him now she appreciated the gesture.

"Babe, if you want to go in with your mother alone, I understand."

"No," Phyllis protested. "I want you to come with me."

Damien nodded and proceeded to the visitor's desk hand-in-hand with his wife. "We're here to see Jonetta Miller," Damien told the woman at the desk. He had been down this very same road before. Thanks to a drunk driver, his parents were both deceased now for seven years. It took him a while to recover from that untimely and unexpected loss. He knew the day would come for Phyllis to lose a parent and he hoped to be the best support system to her as she was to him.

They proceeded to the sterile hospital room where Jonetta lied stiffly. Phyllis froze at the door. She stared at her mother who was unable to speak or even acknowledge their presence and welled up with tears. Phyllis felt her knees give way from underneath her. Damien, always in tune, immediately grabbed her by the waist and held her up.

"Come on, baby. You gotta be strong." He kissed her cheek, urging her to enter the room. "Take a seat over by her bed."

Phyllis swallowed hard, and slowly took seat in the corner instead. She stared at her once vibrant, talkative mother in disbelief.

"Why does she look like that?"

"What do you mean, babe?"

"Stiff, frozen… dead." Phyllis threw her hand over her mouth and began to sob softly. The thought of her mother no longer here on this earth with them scared her shitless. Damien rushed to embrace her.

"She's not dead, baby. She's just finally getting some much needed rest."

"I'm okay. I'm okay, babe." Phyllis stood to her feet and walked to her mother's bedside. She touched her hand; it was cold and unusually frail. Or had Phyllis just not taken notice before? As long as Phyllis could remember, her mother was always just the right weight, never overweight, never skinny. Her hair was always neat, in place, and she always smelled good. She was perfect in that way and expected the same from her three daughters. Much to Jonetta's disappointment, they didn't even come close.

"Phyllis. My first born daughter. I can actually smell your perfume mixed with Damien's cologne."

"Mama, I don't like this one bit. You don't belong here. I'm trying to think of the right things to say to you right now, but I'm so angry that you're even here. How did you allow stress to bring you to stroke level? You know better than that!"

"Phyllis…" Damien interrupted her chastising session. "Baby, ummm… take it easy."

"No," Phyllis countered. "My Mama needs some strong talking to right now! I'm the oldest and she groomed me be to be strong for everyone else. So, I'm about to be strong for her, too."

"Phyllis, I thought you were my eldest child, too. I don't know how you or the other girls will even receive the news. I need to wake up."

Phyllis caressed her mother's face softly. "The doctor said that you should be waking up today. Are you faking it to stay longer? If that's the case, Mama, you can just forget it. Nobody even knows if you have insurance, so you might as well get outta here before they bill you for one-hundred thousand dollars."

Damien chuckled.

"I don't want to be here, trust me. I have no idea why my eyes won't open, baby. Lord knows that I've tried a million times to open them."

"Damien, would you like to talk to Mama?"

He held up his hands and shook his head no. "You're doing a fine job, babe. Keep talking to her. I'm pretty sure she can hear you."

"Well, at least get over here and give her a kiss."

"What? Hell no!"

Damien raised his eyebrows. He didn't even do that on a regular basis while she was well. Phyllis waved him off.

"Anyway, Mama. It's been a whirlwind these past two days. Thankfully, you didn't pass out *during* Aunt Georgia's funeral. That would've been a hoot!" Phyllis laughed.

"My poor sister. What have I done?"

Suddenly, Phyllis's face grew solemn. "With you and Aunt Georgia gone now… things will never be the same again."

"Gone? I'm not gone! Girl, I'm right here. You're so dramatic."

"Babe, things will get back to normal," Damien reassured her. Now standing at her side, he squeezed her shoulders.

His touch sent chills racing down her arms. She let out a sigh and began to cry again. Damien hugged her, allowing her as long as she liked this time.

Back in their SUV, Damien held her onto her thigh as he drove. Occasionally, caressing directly between her thighs. Phyllis leaned her seat back as far as it would go, allowing her husband all the room he needed to explore her body. She closed her eyes and moaned as he caressed her thighs and explored her breasts. This was exactly what she needed. The gentle rocking from the ride lulled her into a light slumber. The halt of the ride broke her sleep and when she opened her eyes she didn't recognize her surroundings.

"Where are we?" she asked, raising her seat upright.

Damien had a sly little grin across his face. "Climb in the back."

"What?" Phyllis shrieked. She peered out the window to get a better look. "Are we at the beach?"

"Yes, now move your seat up some and climb in the back."

Phyllis laughed nervously. "What if we get caught?"

"We have tinted windows." Damien winked at her. "Now go on and get that ass back there."

Phyllis climbed in the back of the SUV as she was told and Damien joined her. He unbuckled his belt, unzipped his pants and gestured for Phyllis to do the same. Luckily, she had on yoga pants so she easily slipped one leg out. As soon as he was in good-seated position, he snatched Phyllis by the arm and placed her right on top of him.

"Come here, baby. Sit on Daddy's lap." He held his erect member in his hand as she slid her moist warmth right on top. Damien moaned loudly as Phyllis repeatedly thrust her hips back and forth.

"You like that, Daddy?"

"Yes! That's right, baby. Fuck your man!"

Phyllis could barely catch her breath at the rhythm she was going. This random sexplosion had completely caught her off guard. The back-to-back orgasms she was experiencing reminded her that she hadn't been on top during sex in a while. She threw her head back, moaned as Damien wrapped his wide hand around her neck.

She took a peek at his face and knew from his expression that he would explode any second so she stopped mid-stroke and slid off quickly.

"Baby, don't stop!" Damien begged. "What are you doing? Get back on top and ride me, please!"

That was enough for the day. "No, and you know why."

Chapter 6

"Dad, I'm here to help. The way I see it, you're here alone and I'm alone over there…"

"I'm at *peace*," Norman remarked quickly. He knew where the conversation was headed. Switching gears he continued, "At the funeral I dropped a tiny bomb on you," Norman admitted.

Colette looked puzzled. "Dad, don't try to change the subject. I'm really at a cross-roads in my life. Well, we all are since Mama is in the hospital. I'm sick of being in that big house all by myself. It's lonely and creepy at times."

"Creepy?"

Colette nodded. "I hear things creaking and it sometimes it sounds like someone is walking in the attic."

"Probably just the house settling."

"If you say so, Dad," Colette exhaled. "The kids really like it here with you."

"I bet they do!"

"Well, so do I," she cooed. "You know that I can cook, clean and we can keep each other company."

"And when your mother comes home from the hospital she will need complete rest as she heals," Norman replied sharply. "Getting your mother back to complete health will be my number one priority."

"So, is that a no?"

Norman shot her a look and decided to switch back to his previous conversation. "About that tiny bomb… You don't remember, do you? Damn! I should've kept my mouth shut, huh?" He laughed heartily.

"Oh, you mean about you being married before? Yeah, that was some brand new news to me."

"Like I was trying to tell you, dissolving a marriage is not easy. It wears on your heart, mind and can cause your spirits to reach an all-time low. Lots of questions swirl around in your head. Like, am I doing the right thing? How will this affect the other person? Am I prepared to start over? You want to make sure you're doing the right thing for *yourself* while trying your best not to maliciously hurt the other person you took vows with. But deep inside you know that you have to move on."

"Who was your first wife? Where is she? Did you all have kids together?"

"Now you know being the father that I am, you would've known if you had other siblings! Give me some credit here."

Colette nodded in agreement. "That's true, Dad."

"My first wife was a good woman. We were so young and only married for about a year or so. I had just got home from the service and I thought that I was doing the right thing by marrying her. She waited on me to return not knowing if I would return or if I'd return in one piece or in my right mind. So for that reason, I married her. Then I met your mother." A sly grin grew across Norman's face as he recalled meeting Jonetta. "I risked it all for that woman. I had survived the war, managed not to get killed and could've been killed right here at home for dealing with your mother. She was in a dangerous situation and desperate to get out. I don't regret a moment of it. Nope. Plus, she gave me three beautiful daughters."

"Wow! I never knew any of that. But unlike you, Dad, I regret ever marrying Owen," Colette admitted.

"Come on now, don't say that. I wouldn't have my four grandchildren if it weren't for him," Norman reminded her. "Always find the lesson in your troubles or else the lesson will just keep repeating itself."

Colette felt her chest tighten as her mind replayed the most recent ferocious moments of their volatile relationship. She rubbed the scar above her left brow as a reminder that their marriage was definitely over. "God knows that I don't want to repeat a life with Owen, ever! Sometimes I just feel worthless. Like I'm a thorn in everyone's side. Only a meal to the babies, and a nanny to the older kids. I feel so alone and unloved." She inhaled sharply as a tear escaped down her cheek. "I've only been with one man and Owen Aldridge ain't even worth the space his name takes up on our divorce papers. He did a number on my heart. I don't know how I'll ever love or trust another man again! I don't know if I even want to, Dad. For what? So he can make a fool of me, too? I'd rather die first than go through that humiliation and pain again."

Norman patted her shoulder and handed her a handkerchief from his pocket. He was so old school in that way. "Calm down, calm down. Listen, you cannot spend the rest of your life in regret. You were young, in love, and doe-eyed for that boy the moment you saw him. There's no crime in that, Colette. You loved at the purest time in your life. You were young, and didn't know any better." Norman laughed at the naivety of young lovers.

"I just want to get this divorce over with so I can be free."

"Alright then. Get your divorce. Let your heart heal and most of all, forgive yourself." Norman patted Colette's knee gently.

"Forgive myself?"

"Yes, forgive yourself for not loving *you* more."

Tears spilled from her eyes down her plump cheeks. Norman scooted closer and embraced his daughter, allowing her tears to stain his neatly pressed, navy blue button down shirt. When they peeled apart, Norman wiped her tears away and looked down at his shirt.

"Now it looks like I'm breastfeeding!"

"Dad!" Colette nudged him, laughing.

"There's that smile! Keep smiling, sweetheart. This is just a bump in the road on your journey. It'll be alright."

Chapter 7

Breakfast at the Franklyn's often consisted of black coffee and buttered wheat toast. Barbara was no chef in the kitchen, God bless her soul, but she managed not to burn the hash browns and scrambled eggs with tomatoes, spinach and feta cheese this early morning. They had always been early risers, even when Bishon was a child. The weekends were no exceptions.

Barbara firmly believed in conquering Saturdays early with chores or errands and afternoons were for pampering and fine dining. She put the chores on hold this morning to make sure that Bishon had her undivided attention. There weren't many chores to do around the house because when Bishon graduated from college, they downgraded to a smaller, ranch-style home with two bedrooms. Not having any steps to climb anymore was better on their knees and there were less chances they would have a slip and fall accident.

Fully dressed, well-rested and with breakfast ready, Barbara was ready to see her son's face.

"Stanton!" Barbara called down the hallway. "Bishon will be here any moment. What are you doing?"

"Can a man breathe?" Stanton grumbled as he emerged from their bedroom. "I'm coming! I'm coming!"

Normally, Barbara was calm and mild-mannered, but today she was anxious for the news that her only child had to share.

"I hope he tells us that he found the right woman to marry. I'm so ready for grandchildren," Barbara confessed.

Stanton chuckled, "You are, sweetheart?"

A huge smile spread across Barbara's face as she poured two cups of freshly brewed coffee into matching mugs. "Yes, I am, thank you very much."

"You know that means no more afternoon teas at the Peninsula with your girlfriends. No more pampering at The Red Door spa. No more shopping on the Magnificent Mile just because the spirit moves you…"

"Excuse me, but why does my life have to change just because I'll have a few grandchildren?"

Stanton laughed boisterously and the doorbell rang. "I'll get the door." He excused himself to greet Bishon.

"Morning son!" Stanton embraced Bishon and led him to the kitchen. "You can always use your key, ya know?"

"Morning, Dad. That key is for emergencies only," he reminded him. "I would hate to alarm you and get shot!"

Stanton laughed and waved him off. "Sweetheart, look who I found at the front door."

Barbara gave him a long, warm hug. She cupped his face with her hands and cooed, "My son. How are you?"

"I'm well, Mom," he planted a kiss on her cheek. Making his way to the cabinets, he grabbed his favorite mug from and poured a cup of coffee. "Smells like you cooked in here."

Barbara blushed, "I did and I hope you like it."

Bishon lifted the pot lids and smiled when he saw the food. It actually looked appetizing. Unfortunately, his stomach was in knots and couldn't manage food right now. But the proud look on his mother's face prompted him to pull plates from the cabinet anyway.

"I can make your plate," Barbara offered.

"No, I got it Mom," Bishon replied. He knew they were going to need a lot of strength after he shared his news.

Halfway through small bites and small talk about opening his new dental location, Bishon cleared his throat to tell them the news that he needed to share. "So, Mom, you know that I love you and you will always be my number one girl, right?"

Barbara beamed and gave Stanton a glare that screamed: *"I told you so!"*
"Yes, son, of course," Barbara replied, squeezing his hand for reassurance. "So, who is she?"
Wow! This is going to be easier than I thought, Bishon said to himself as he sat back in his chair. "Jonetta Miller."
Stanton dropped his fork onto his plate, making a clanking sound loud enough for the neighbor's dog to start barking.
"Son, what the hell are you talking about?"
Barbara gasped and placed her mug down slowly. "You're in love with Jonetta Miller?"
"What!?" Bishon knitted his eyebrows together. "Mom, what on earth are *you* talking about?"
They all sat in silence confused for an awkward moment. Barbara looked back and forth between the two men in her life and explained, "Well, I thought you were going to tell us that… that you found a woman…finally."
"Well, I did…sort of…but… No, I'm not in love with Jonetta Miller!" Bishon vehemently denied, shaking his head.
"Then what *are* you talking about?" Stanton asked frustrated.
Bishon sighed and leaned back slowly as he gauged his parent's anticipation. "Listen, I wanted to share news with you about finding my birth mother."
"Oh!" Barbara said. She was relieved momentarily until the realization of his words finally sunk into her thoughts. "Oh… wait a minute! You mean… are you telling us that Jonetta is your… birth mother?"
"Mom, like I said before you will always be my number one girl. Nobody will ever take your place." He scooted his chair closer to Barbara to console her. "Yes, Jonetta is my birth mother."
"But… Wait a minute. Aren't you dating her daughter? What's her name?" Barbara asked bewildered.
Bishon nodded, "Dawn. Yes, we were getting serious, but now…"
"Oh, my God!" Barbara covered her mouth.
"Son, I'm sorry. I really don't know what to say about that."
Stanton threw his hands in the air and shook his head.
"Me neither, Dad." Bishon dropped his head in shame.
"Have you spoken to Dawn? Norman? Anybody?" Stanton asked desperately.

Bishon shook his head. "I tried to talk to Dawn, but… she's avoiding me for some strange reason."

"Wow! She's your half-sister." Norman stated the obvious.

"Do you think she knows?" Barbara asked rejoining the conversation.

"I doubt that," Bishon replied. "I only told Jonetta, then she fell to the ground, and now…she's suffering from a stroke."

They sat in another moment in awkward silence.

"Well, on the bright side, I'm glad you finally found out who your mother is, son. Lucky for you, she's still alive, ya know?" Stanton wrapped his knuckles on the marble table, his staple move ever since he binged watched *House of Cards* on Netflix.

Barbara shot a harsh yet hurtful look towards Stanton. "How can you say that?"

"Because our son was in anguish trying to find his mother!"

"*I'm* his mother!" Barbara said fiercely and excused herself from the table.

"Mom!" Bishon called out to her but she had already disappeared down the hallway and slammed the bedroom door.

Chapter 8

Colette swung the front door to their father's house open wide, and greeted her sisters and nieces as they piled in for dinner. Everyone was assigned a dish to bring. Usually, there was a theme for dinner: Italian, Soul Food, Asian, Mexican, Greek, or traditional American. Not this time. Colette told them to bring whatever they like. Even the children had options about what they wanted to eat.

"No Damien today?" Norman asked.

"Nope. He didn't want to miss the game." Phyllis shrugged.

"We could've snuck away together to catch at least the second half."

Phyllis placed her hand up, "Not good enough, Dad. That man loves him some football, undisturbed."

"I guess he's not protesting the NFL, huh?" Norman asked.

Phyllis pursed her lips, shot her dad a look and headed towards the kitchen.

"And he didn't want to be the only man. You know, since Colette and I no longer have men," Dawn added.

"Who am I? Chop liver?" Norman countered.

Phyllis rolled her eyes at Dawn. "No, Dad. It's not like that. Don't take it personal."

"Well, more food for me!" Norman conceded.

Ready to dig in, the sisters set the table quickly. Norman was grateful that he had purchased a 10-person dining room set a few years ago. He had a feeling that if he just remained consistent with being part of the family that it would be put to good use. Goosebumps raced up his arms as he looked around the table and saw his grandchildren's beaming faces, and the delicious foods his daughters' prepared. His heart was full.

"Let's say grace," Colette suggested.

Norman cleared the knot out of his throat to begin, but Cornell interrupted and asked to lead the prayer.

"Go ahead, son." Colette beamed with pride at her nine-year-old son who looked more like his father as he grew older. He was going to turn out just fine, her heart had already told her so.

They all held hands and bowed as he prayed.

"Everything tastes so good, girls," Norman gushed scarfing down a spoonful of macaroni and cheese. His plate was piled fried catfish, baked chicken thighs, collard greens, oven baked macaroni and cheese, and sweet potatoes.

"Make sure you taste my zucchini and yellow squash, Dad." Phyllis eyed his plate. He had a heap of everyone's food on his plate except hers. After all these years that competitive jealous streak of hers always had a way of showing up whenever they all gathered as a family.

"I will," he reassured her. "I just don't like the juices flowing on the rest of my food. I need a bowl or a saucer or something."

"It's a 'Viewers' Choice' on my cooking channel. They love it and I'm sure you will, too." Phyllis reached across the table, grabbed a saucer and plopped a heap of vegetables on it. "Pass this to your grandpa." She instructed to Cornell.

Norman chuckled accepting the saucer and gave Phyllis a wink.

"This just isn't the same without Mama being here," Dawn admitted, unapologetically, and placed her fork down on the table.

"You need to eat," Norman replied, eyeing his youngest daughter sternly. She got the message and stuffed macaroni and cheese in her mouth.

"I'm praying that Mama will be home soon," Colette replied.

"I know she will because she's a fighter," Phyllis replied. "And I told her to open her eyes and get on out that hospital before they kill her!"

"Phyllis!" Colette exclaimed. "Don't be so dramatic, especially in front of the kids."

"Well, I'm glad you had a chance to visit your mother yesterday," Norman interjected before they began to bicker. "Dawn, when will you get a chance to visit your mother?"

"Tomorrow, definitely." Dawn replied, nodding her head. "I'm missing my Mama right now. I need her more now than I ever have."

Colette glanced at Phyllis confused by their sister's statement, but Phyllis shrugged her shoulders in return.

"I miss my grandma, too." Cornell admitted as he stabbed a fork into a thick slice of ham.

"That's *my* grandma!" Serena remarked, sneering at her cousin.

"No! That's *my* grandma!" Lydia countered.

Phyllis clinked her fork on her wine glass to cease the petty argument ensuing amongst the cousins. It worked.

The alarm sensor chimed, followed by the doorbell.

"Saved by the bell, huh?" Dawn said giving a stern look to all the kids at the table.

"Are you expecting someone other than your daughters?" Phyllis asked Norman raising her eyebrows.

"Not at all." Norman stood up from the head of the table, wiped his mouth with a napkin and headed to the front door.

"Stanton, how's it going, man?" Norman stepped aside, allowing his old friend in the house. "Come on in! You're just in time if you're starving. I've got my daughters over here and they've cooked up a storm for Sunday dinner."

"No, I'm fine, thank you." Stanton exhaled and shot his eyes towards the polished, cherry wood floor.

"Everything alright, man?" Norman placed his thick hand on his friend's frail shoulder. Until now, he never noticed how thin Stanton was underneath all of his clothes.

Stanton rubbed his smooth chin. "Listen, I wish there was a much better way to tell you this…"

"Dad! Who is it?" Phyllis called from the dining room.

They both looked towards the direction of the chatter. Norman shook his head and waved her off.

"Actually, it's probably no better time to tell you since the family is all here. The news I have to share…everyone in the family should hear."

"Everyone?" Norman asked. "Well, if that's the case, I hope it's good news." But something told Norman that it wasn't good news at all. He had just called the hospital to check on Jonetta a few hours before his daughters arrived, so it couldn't be about her.

Phyllis appeared in the hallway and flashed a polite smile. "Hello, Mr. Stanton. Looks like we spoke you up!"

"Is that right?" he remarked. "How are you, Phyllis?" Stanton forced a smile and wrinkles appeared around the corners of his eyes. He directed his attention to the twins peering around the corner. He waved, "Hi there, little ones. I see you."

Phyllis turned around to see the twins. She pursed her lips and placed a fist on her hip, "Well, are you going to speak to Mr. Stanton or just stare?"

The twins waved, snickered and fled back to the dining room.

Phyllis turned her attention back to Stanton, shaking her head. "Are you joining us for dinner?" We have plenty of food."

Stanton shook his head. "No, thank you, though."

Norman didn't miss the melancholy tone of his friend's voice. "Phyllis, give us a moment," Norman said, placing his hand her shoulder. "I'll be back at the table soon. Don't wait on me to finish eating."

"Oh, we won't, Dad," Phyllis chuckled. "Good seeing you, Mr. Stanton."

He nodded and swallowed hard. Norman led him to the living room where Jonetta had added flair with tall plants in every corner. Norman had a cream and forest green colored theme going until Jonetta added burnt orange throw pillows with a touch of gold threading that added the right amount of sparkle to the ambience especially when the sunlight filled the room.

"On second thought, it's probably best I just share the news with you since the children are here, too." Stanton shoved his hands into his pants that seemed to swallow him up.

"Have a seat, man." Norman said directing him to the love seat. "Tell me what's going on."

"I apologize for just popping up over here, but I just had to talk to you man-to-man…you know… face-to-face about this since we're friends," Stanton began. "The timing is awful since Jonetta is still hospitalized. But…oh, man, I realized this is probably exactly why she suffered a stroke. I know that I almost did, too, when I found out." He shook his head, scratching the back of his neck.

Norman knitted his brows together with concern. He sat back in his favorite forest green leather chair, waiting patiently for his friend to spit out whatever it is he needed to get off his chest.

Stanton searched his friend's face and exhaled. "You know my son, Shon…Bishon, has been on a quest to find his birth mother."

Norman nodded and grunted.

"Well, he succeeded."

"Good for him!" Norman leaned forward and slapped his friend on his knee.

Stanton scoffed. "Depends on who you ask, man."

Norman sat back puzzled. "What do you mean, man? Is Barbara upset about it? I could understand if she is, you know. She'll always be his mother, no matter what though."

Stanton raised his eyebrows and shook his head. He buried his face in his frail hands and began to rub his temples. "Jonetta is his birth mother."

"What did you just say, man?" Norman clenched his jaws repeatedly.

Stanton inhaled sharply, looked his friend in the eyes and repeated his revelation.

Norman shot to his feet, mumbled a few curse words and sat back down. He rubbed his salt and pepper beard as his thoughts raced. "What? How? Are you sure? Is he absolutely sure?"

"Shon is positive. He did a lot of research and it led back to that house where Jonetta grew up with her two aunts."

"Unbelievable. Do you know what this will mean for Jonetta? For our family?"

"Jonetta already knows about it."

"What the hell are you talking about?" Norman asked with his mouth twisted in a challenge. "If she knew about this, I guarantee you that she would've told me!"

"I don't doubt that," Stanton agreed. "Like I said before, I believe this news is exactly why Jonetta had the stroke."

Stanton explained the timing of when Bishon shared the news with her at the funeral and soon after, she suffered a stroke. It was making sense to Norman just how news like that could take Jonetta out at her sister's funeral. Then again, it wasn't making sense to him based on everything Jonetta had told him about her first pregnancy.

"Her aunts… No, no, no…" Norman stood, wagging his finger pacing the living room. "Her aunts buried her stillborn son. That's what they told her… that he died and they buried him in the yard underneath that damn mulberry tree."

"I don't know anything about that, man. All I know is Bishon is Jonetta's son." Stanton replied matter-of-factly. "The son she thought was stillborn ended up on our church doorstep in a damn box. Honestly, I knew all along that the baby came from a whore house… I mean… uhhh…the aunt's residence." Stanton cleared his throat.

Norman waved him off. "It's okay, man. It is what it is. I loved Jonetta anyway. I've always loved her regardless of her circumstances as a prostitute. I left my first wife for her. I rescued her from that pimp and I had a whole family with her. Trust me, it's okay. But, you knew that part this whole time? Did Barbara know that, too?"

Stanton shook his head. "No, I never told her that. We were desperately trying to have our own child, but it just wasn't working. We didn't have all these options that these folks have nowadays when they want a baby, ya know? Barbara would've rejected the baby if she knew it came from a loose woman." His face filled with regret the moment the words left his lips.

Norman waved him off again.

"I'm sorry. I should've never told Bishon that I knew that part, but he was so desperate to know who his birth mother was and I hated seeing him struggle with it." Stanton admitted. "This is just a complete mess now." Stanton gave his friend a moment to let his confession sink in before he dropped the next bomb.

Norman continued to pace. He stopped abruptly and turned his attention towards the dining room.

Stanton sighed, following his gaze. “So you know what this means for your daughters, right?”

“Shit!” Norman replied punching his fist into his hand. “They have a damn brother!”

“Yes, and…Dawn and Shon were getting pretty serious…”

Norman threw his hands in the air. “Say no more, Stanton. Say no more. Damn!”

“Shon hasn’t told her yet.”

Norman spun around to face his friend. The realization punched him right in the gut. “And I’m sure Dawn hasn’t told him the news yet, either.”

“Told him what news?” Stanton stood to his feet swiftly.

“She’s pregnant.”

Stanton fell back onto the sofa as if a strong gust of wind pushed him. He groaned and clutched at his sides. “Oh, my God.”

Norman turned to look up at the sky and exhaled. “God, you gotta help me out with this one.”

Chapter 9

"You had no right telling anybody!" Barbara said fiercely through clenched teeth.

"What's the big deal? They were going to find out soon or later."

"It wasn't your business to tell!"

Stanton hung his head. Maybe she was right. No, he knew that she was right as she usually was about these things. Barbara was far more calculated and patient. She had even waited on him to propose after dating her for almost nine years. Back in those days, it was unheard of for a man to court a woman that long. But she waited patiently on him to come to his senses.

Stanton truly loved Barbara, but he wasn't done sniffing up other skirts. There were beautiful women migrating up north to Chicago just about every month it seemed. He wanted to show all of them a good time, until two women pulled a knife on him to rob him. That's when he knew that he was done with the fast life and fast women.

Marrying Barbara was the smartest thing he had done for his life. She was a good woman, steady with her love and supportive of the two men in her life. She was uniquely beautiful with exaggerated features that only her face could wear. Her complexion was honey-dipped, always glowing and youthful. She dressed modestly, yet with a classy flair and that's what Stanton loved about her style.

Although he married her during her child bearing years, she was unable to have any children. When Stanton found a baby boy on the steps of their church, he knew that whatever love that baby was missing, Barbara would give it to him.

Bishon was their son, no matter how it came about. They raised him in the admonition of the Lord, respectfully and whole-heartedly loved him as their own. Even as a boy, Bishon was always eager to please his parents. It came to no surprise that he became a successful dentist. He was a natural scholar, immersing himself in his studies, never a playboy. The young girls were very fond of him, but they soon lost interest when they realized that he was focused on a career instead of a family.

These past few years, Barbara had been hinting that she needed grandchildren in her life, but the last two women he brought around were "not good enough" for him. Stanton reminded him to take his time because once he committed to one woman, she would want the world, and he had better be ready to give it to her.

Stanton held up the wall in their lavish dining room and exhaled. Maybe he did jump the gun this time, but it was too much of a burden to bear. Bishon was dragging his feet telling Dawn the news, so he felt like it was time to drop the bomb on the whole family. Yet, he was the one who left stunned.

"Be that as it may, I'm glad that I did," Stanton admitted.

"Are you really? We'll see if you feel the same way when Bishon finds out that you told his business *before* he had the opportunity." Barbara snapped and walked away quickly to the kitchen. She headed straight for the wine rack and grabbed a bottle of Shiraz.

"You don't even know the half of it," Stanton replied, following her into their kitchen slowly.

"I'm listening," Barbara said as she poured a full glass of wine.

Stanton reached for his bottle of Bullet Whiskey and poured a few ounces more than usual. He took a sip before he began. "This news is worse than Bishon finding his birth mother."

"What could be worse than replacing *me*?"

"You can never be replaced, sweetheart."

"Then what could be worse than incest?"

Stanton dropped his eyes towards his glass, his mind searched for a gentle way to break more terrible news to his already emotional wife.

"Well?" Barbara took another swallow of wine and waited for Stanton to spill the beans.

"Dawn is pregnant." Now it was his turn to take a swallow.

Barbara choked on her wine, bent over the sink, and coughed until she caught her breath. Stanton patted her on the back forcefully until she twisted her body away from his reach.

"Sweetheart, are you alright? I'm sorry… I'm so sorry. I know this is just getting worse by the minute."

When her eyes met his they were full of tearful confusion. "This is unbelievable! Don't say another word, Stanton."

"Come on and sit down, sweetheart, please."

"You should've told me to do that in the first place!"

Stanton grimaced. She was right, again.

Chapter 10

The drama with the men in her life is what caused her mother collapse in the first place. At least that's what she told herself. Although, the doctors determined that it was stress that contributed to the stroke, Dawn couldn't help but be riddled with guilt. Dawn knew that she was being reckless sleeping with two men at the same time, but she also didn't believe in birth control pills. Pumping her body with poison to prevent pregnancy was unnatural and unhealthy according to Dawn. The one thing she prided herself on was eating healthy and staying away from pills. That little stint in New York with cocaine was just to fit in with the crowd. At times, she missed that cocaine high racing through her body, but for now she was satisfied with Sativa.

A knot in her stomach made her inhale sharply. She placed her hand over belly and closed her eyes. "I don't know if that's you in there making me feel nauseous or this hospital." The stench of sickness and cleanser traveled through her nose as she walked through the hospital corridors. She quickly looked for a lemon drop candy in her purse and popped it in her mouth. Just as the popular pregnancy blog suggested, they really helped combat nausea. Yes, it had come down to low-key reading pregnancy blogs. After all, she was going through the motions of pregnancy even though she was undecided about her next move.

The security doors whooshed open and Dawn slowed her pace as she approached the nurses' station. *What is she doing on this floor?* Immediately, she recognized one of the nurses from the oncology department where she would take her best friend, Chena, to her appointments. It was definitely that nurse with the bubbly personality, blemish-free peanut butter skin, always sporting braids or twists, with a big ole booty and eyes like pools of honey. There was always something about that nurse that Dawn didn't particularly care for, but she couldn't put her finger on it. Dawn cleared her throat and only two nurses looked up from their computers.

Immediately, the nurse recognized Dawn and flashed a smile. "Hi, there. Aren't you on the wrong floor?"

"Funny, I was just thinking the same about you." Dawn replied, raising her perfectly arched eyebrows.

"Nope, I'm floating today," she replied. "What brings you to the ICU floor? Is everything alright with your friend, Mrs. Wilson?"

Dawn smirked. "Chena. Yes, she's fine. You remembered her name?"

"Yes, of course, I remember all of my oncology patients." She rounded the corner of the station with an electronic chart pad in hand. "And her husband, Raffi."

Just the mention of his name made Dawn throb between her legs. A familiar throb, especially when she knew that he was about to blow her mind in bed, or in the hallway, car or wherever he felt like fucking her. That's it. That's why she didn't like this nurse. She was too familiar with him. Too flirty. Too close. Always offering him something to drink, bringing him tissue when he squeezed tears from his eyes, being a listening ear. *No, bitch you just remember Chena because you were probably fucking her husband.* Even now, this bitch just referred to him by first name. A tinge of jealousy shot through Dawn. She shook her head of thoughts of stabbing the nurse with a needle right in her jugular. Raffi's dick was community property. He was nobody's man, not even Chena's.

"Actually, I'm here to see my mother, Mrs. Miller, in room one thirty-two." Dawn flipped her curly hair over shoulder and in that moment, she was glad that she put effort into her appearance today.

"Oh, she's not my patient. But I do hope she recovers soon." She replied, placing a hand on Dawn's shoulder.

Dawn shot darts at the nurse with her dark eyes and the nurse immediately removed her hand and walked away.

"Mrs. Miller is my patient," a young, Asian male nurse with a man-bun announced. He stood and extended his hand towards Dawn. "You can call me Niko."

Dawn reluctantly shook his hand. "Any updates?"

"I'll walk with you," he offered, grabbing his electronic chart pad and escorted Dawn towards her mother's room. "Actually, your mother is showing signs of improvement and we think in a few days she can leave ICU, but not the hospital. Your mother would need to do some therapy and…"

Dawn interrupted, "What types of improvement?"

"She's responding to sensitivity now. We also believe she can hear us based on her heart rate." Niko chuckled and nodded his head.

Dawn wasn't amused.

They stopped at the doorway and held a stare. *What the hell is so funny? This is my mother's life you're snickering about.* Dawn was growing irritated by the minute.

"Well, what does the *doctor* say?" Dawn asked intentionally as an insult.

"Exactly what I'm telling you," Niko retorted. "I can page him if you like."

"That won't be necessary." Dawn conceded. She wanted to be alone with her mother. "Thanks for the update."

When Dawn entered the room, seeing her mother laid up, incapable of speaking, sadness swept over her. She hung her black Valentino purse on the back of the door, grabbed a chair and pulled next to her mother's bedside.

"Mama, I don't know if you can even hear me or not, but I'm here." Dawn squeezed her mother's hand. It was cold, yet flexible. "Are these even enough blankets for you? You'll end up having pneumonia before you leave this damn cold hospital."

"Tell me about it, baby girl."

"I can't stand seeing you like this. I swear to God!" Dawn whimpered. She scanned the room looking at all the tubes, machines beeping and whirring, and wanted to roll her mother right out of that hospital on the gurney. She wanted her mother back home desperately.

"I still don't even know what happened to you, Mama. I know you were under a lot of stress with your only sister dying. Then with all of our drama making matters worse. None of us have been living right and we know you taught us better. We're gonna do better, Mama. I promise. "

"My poor baby. I hope you don't end up having a stroke once you find out the mess you're in now."

"I'm so sorry that I wasn't at the funeral," Dawn continued, whispering. "I was on my way, I swear, but… I should've just listened to your advice, Mama. I'm so stupid! I should've never told Raffi anything! He damn near killed me!"

"What?!"

"That's why my eyes are red. They're getting a little better every day though. I've been telling everyone that it's because I've been crying over you being here and Aunt Georgia dying. I just can't bring myself to tell anyone that truth. But… yeah, if I was going to tell the truth, it's because Raffi almost choked the life out of me when I told him that he wasn't the only one I had slept with lately. He flipped the fuck out!"

"Oh, hell no! Tell your Dad so he can send somebody to whoop his ass!"

"Oops! Sorry about that, Mama." Dawn threw her hand over her mouth. "I know, I know. You warned me that I was playing with fire by being his helpful handmaid and that I shouldn't tell him anything about this pregnancy. I didn't mean for any of that to happen. I was just trying to help Chena while she battled cancer. That's where I should've drawn the line. I know! But, she didn't mind and all that curiosity that was built up over these past years between me and Raffi… and… Well, we just couldn't help ourselves."

"You mean neither of you cared about anybody but yourselves and helped yourselves to yourselves! What a mess you've made, girl."

"Anyway, Mama, I'm babbling. Thankfully, his son, Shiloh, came to my rescue. Then I got the hell outta there and drove straight to the funeral. That's when I saw you in the parking lot talking to Bishon and then… then… you just hit the ground."

"God, I know you hear me! I feel closer to you more now than ever before. Things have gone way too far! You've got to wake me up so I can fix things with my family! She is going to snap when she learns the truth about Bishon. I need to be there for her, God. Please!"

Dawn rested her head on her mother's arm. "Mama, please wake up. What am I supposed to do? I'm so scared. For the first time in my life I truly feel lost and alone." Dawn lamented.

The increasing rapid sound of the heart monitor caught Dawn's attention. She popped her head up and squinted her eyes at the numbers. "Mama, your heart is beating faster. You can hear me, can't you?"

"Of course, I can, baby."

"Well, just calm down. I'm going to be okay. We need *you* to be okay. Take some deep breaths, Mama. This machine is beeping too fast. It's making me nervous." Dawn stroked her mother's hand softly and said a silent prayer. A few moments passed and the beeping sound reduced to a normal pace. A smile crept across Dawn's face as she kissed her mother's hand. "That's better, Mama. We can't have the family blaming me for your setback!"

"Well, don't tell me nothing else to get my blood pressure up!"

"Don't worry about my pregnancy. I'll work things out on my own with this baby. Get better, Mama. We need you."

"You're pregnant?"

Dawn snapped her head around to face that familiar voice. It was Bishon.

What the hell are you doing here? Dawn sprung to her feet. She eyed him up and down; he sported a tailored navy blue suit and had a colorful bouquet of flowers in his hand. His cologne wafted into the room and the heart rate monitor began beeping faster.

Dawn turned her attention to the monitor and then her mother. She squeezed her cold hand again and placed her other hand on top of her forehead. "Mama, I'll be right back." Dawn planted a quick kiss on her cheek. She snatched her purse from the hook on the door, placed a hand on Bishon's chest pushing him back into the hallway, ultimately forcing him out of the room.

"Dawn, wait a minute…" Bishon protested, taking a few steps back. "You're pregnant?" His voice hit a high octave and his eyes frantically searched her face.

Dawn looked around nervously. "Would you please lower your voice?" She stormed off down the hallway that lead into main waiting area.

Bishon followed her woodenly down the hall with his mouth open and eyes wild.

"Slow down, Dawn. We really need to talk!"

Dawn eyed the waiting room for an empty space. A young white girl sat mindlessly staring out the window while a tall, lanky man, who seemed to be her father, offered words of encouragement. A middle-aged Latino man in a suit sat against the wall, scrolling through his phone. The opposite side of the waiting room was empty. Dawn sat down quickly before anyone could claim the space. Bishon sat directly across from her, gently placed the flowers in the empty seat next to him and waited for Dawn to speak first. The silence was thick and heavy, filling the space between them.

Dawn mashed her lips together hard enough to feel her teeth making their mark. The cologne she once loved smelling on him was now making her sick on the stomach. She glanced down at her hands as if they held all the answers. This was not how she wanted to break the news to Bishon, especially while visiting her mother in the hospital. How long had he been standing there? She had no idea why he was even there to begin with. Just like when he was at Aunt Georgia's funeral and at the hospital the night her mother was admitted. For what? There was a time the very sight of him excited her. As of late, his presence was annoying her.

Bishon exhaled and sat back. The nervous energy between them had their eyes diverting instead of locking like they usually did.

He began, "Listen…"

"Are you following me?" Dawn interrupted.

Bishon scoffed. "What? Don't be ridiculous!"

"We were supposed to meet later. *After* I saw my mother, remember?"

"That was two days ago, Dawn. You blew me off. So, here we are now. Let's talk about this pregnancy." Bishon insisted, twisting his lips. He raised his eyebrows expectantly.

Dawn broke his gaze, ran her fingers through her curls and shook her head.

"Take your time," Bishon said sarcastically.

"If you're not following me, what are you doing here?" Dawn retorted.

"I'll get to that in a minute." Bishon glanced over at the flowers, nervously shaking his foot.

"Yes, I'm pregnant. There's your answer. Now, tell me what you are doing here visiting *my* mother."

Bishon groaned and squirmed in his seat. What bothered him the most right now was her tone that implied Jonetta only belonged to her. Dawn also had a flippant attitude about carrying a life inside of her that could possibly be his child. The thought sickened him knowing it could be the ultimate demise of this family. His lust for Dawn led them to this point. He should've used protection. He knew better. But, Dawn had an ethereal vibe that often put him under her spell. It was something deliciously enticing about her and he wanted to experience every inch of her. Even in that moment, he began to grow erect, but combatted his rise with the hard truth. They were siblings.

He knew his announcement was not going to sit well with her. She was never in competition with her sisters, being the baby of the family she was spoiled in that way. The attention was all hers and she knew it. Another sibling to add to the mix would take away her limelight, however. Someone who could potentially be the new apple of their mother's eye, taking away all the attention from her unstable life. Bishon had suffered long enough, waited all of his life to finally meet the woman who gave him life and he wasn't about to feel guilty about it. She would just have to adjust her spoiled ways, as would the other sisters.

His silence sent the wrong message.

"Don't worry. I'm not keeping the baby," Dawn said after a few moments of silence.

Bishon shot her an approving look. "When were you going to tell me? Scratch that! *Why* haven't you told me about this?"

Dawn shrugged and glared down at her feet.

Bishon sighed. He knew he wasn't going to get real answers from Dawn. He clasped his hands together and leaned forward, "I think not keeping the baby is best… for everyone."

"Everyone?" Dawn countered. "Everyone like who?"

"Your whole family... including mine."

"What the hell are you talking about?" Dawn squinted her eyes. "How are *my* pregnancy decisions affecting the whole damn family? Our parents are only friends for crying out loud! We're not related!"

Bishon exhaled sharply, rubbed his forehead and leaned forward to explain. "Dawn, there's no other way to say this. I'm here visiting because I feel responsible for the stroke."

"How?" Dawn furrowed her eyebrows.

"I finally discovered that Jonetta is *my* mother, too."

Chapter 11

Pearly clumps of cum glistened on top of her caramel-kissed belly as she lied on her back trying to catch her breath. Damien had been resentfully pulling out of his wife for the past two years since she was adamant about not having any more kids after their twins reached the age of three-years-old. Phyllis claimed that they kept her busy enough and there was no since in adding to her chaos on a daily basis. Although Damien longed for a son, he obliged his wife to make her happy. That method was certainly working in her favor.

It wasn't an agreement nor an arrangement. It was more as if Phyllis demanded that her husband release his seed anywhere except inside of her. Damien suggested using condoms instead of snatching himself out of her warmth at his climax. She refused. A married man carrying condoms? She might as well had given him permission to cheat as far as she was concerned. The other day, in the back of his truck, they slipped up and immediately afterwards she checked her ovulation calculator app on her phone. They were safe. She was two days past her ovulation date, thankfully.

When her breathing returned to normal, she dabbed her fingertips in the clumps and quickly massaged some in her cheeks and forehead. A smirk crept across her face when she felt it dry into a thin crust. She read somewhere that semen helps tightens the skin, make it feel softer and can even add a glow thanks to the vitamins found in it. Since she was in her mid-thirties it was time to begin a skin care regimen before it was too late. It is true what they say, "Black don't crack", but Phyllis was on the lighter end of the spectrum so she needed all the help that she could get. She closed her eyes, dabbed and massage repeatedly until it was almost gone from her belly.

Damien opened their master bathroom door with a wet, steamy face towel in his hands ready to wipe down his wife only to find her putting it all over her face.

"Babe, what the hell?" Damien laughed. "If you wanted a facial or pearl necklace, I could certainly do it for you."

Phyllis narrowed her eyes and scowled. "Hell would have to freeze over before I let you cum on my face, Damien Xavier Washington. I'm your wife! Not a skanky-hoe from Instagram. I'm simply keeping my skin tight this way. Thank you very much."

Damien stood over her stark naked with a slight erection and handed her the face towel. Phyllis snatched it from him, a tad embarrassed that he caught her in the act of her "skin regimen". He cocked his head to the side as he watched his semen dry on her face quickly. "We should make a video of how this works on your skin. If it really does work, we can bottle up my sperm and sell it… since you don't want it inside of you. Might as well make a killing off of it." He shrugged and smirked.

"Why are you standing over me?" Phyllis jerked her neck, sneered and shooed him away. "Can you move out of my way?"

"No. I want to see how my wife uses every inch of me," he replied, enjoying what he saw. "It's actually a turn on."

Phyllis quickly glanced down to see his erection saluting her at full attention. "Oh, no thanks," she shook her head and tried to roll over before he caught her by the nape of her neck.

"Where are you going?" he asked huskily. "Come here."

Phyllis tried to wiggle away, but his grip was firm. "Babe, please, I don't have time for another round," she pleaded, thinking about the mounting pile of laundry waiting on her not to mention the meal prepping she had to do for her live streaming in a few hours.

"Shhhh…" he placed his fingertip on her supple lips and guided her head closer to him. Damien took the tip of his penis and glided it across her lips as if he were perfectly applying lipstick. "Taste me, babe."

Phyllis knew it wasn't the best time to tell him that she hated giving him oral sex, but it was her best bet to never do it again. She mashed her lips together and shook her head. "No, I don't want to do it. I don't even like doing it."

Damien released his grip in disbelief.

Her confession worked.

"What the hell?" he asked almost stumbling backwards. "Since when?"

Phyllis sat up in their king-sized bed, smoothed her hair and exhaled. She noticed his erection was deflating along with his ego. The once warm damp face towel was now cold as the vibes between them. She placed it on the nightstand and cleared her throat.

Damien walked to their dresser and snatched some underwear from the top drawer, suddenly feeling naked and ashamed. He quickly slid his legs through his boxers and pulled them up.

"Well?" he demanded an answer.

Phyllis waved him off, "It doesn't matter, Damien."

"It matters to me!" he countered, folding his arms across his chest. "First, you insist that I pull out. Do you know how that makes me feel as a man? We're married for God's sake! My own wife doesn't even want me to cum inside of her! You'd rather smear it all over your face!"

"Would you lower your voice?" Phyllis hissed.

"Now you don't want to give me *head* anymore?" Damien continued his rant, ignoring her plea to lower his voice. "What type of shit is that?"

Phyllis leaped from the bed, ran into their bathroom and slammed the door behind her. It was the only way she was going to end the conversation. What did it matter to him that she didn't enjoy sucking on him anymore? What mattered was that he had eight good years of it and should appreciate that. If the spirit moved her in the future, she'd indulge him, but only on her terms.

That afternoon, Phyllis stopped sorting through fresh laundry to eye her husband. She tried to gauge his mood, but figured he was still pissed off from the morning. There was no denying that even if he was mad at her, he was so damned handsome. Even without his long locs that used to cascade down his back. His natural curl pattern gave him a younger, fresher look and his full sandy brown beard sparkled.

If you asked her, Damien should be thanking her for chopping his locs off in his sleep because he looks so much better. It was a low-down dirty move on her part, but she blamed the vodka. Her anger always got the best of her. She couldn't help it. The thoughts swirling around in her head at the possibility of Damien being with another woman only amplified her anger. Bodily harm is what she wanted to do to him, but she didn't want to go to jail.

In hindsight, she should've just had the maturity to simply ask her husband about being seen with Shante, the same bitch who was now Owen's side chick and baby mama. Phyllis should've known that Damien would never stoop that low, but her rage got the better of her.

Since her mother had been in the hospital, Damien had been supportive and loving, which in turn, made her want to be softer towards him. Although, becoming a calmer version of herself was going to take some time. She hoped that she and Damien could get on the same wavelength sooner than later. Damien grabbed his gym bag, pecked her on the cheek and left without saying a word. The best way for her not to get into her feelings was to prepare for her cooking show. As she prepared for her afternoon live stream, she reminded herself to place her phone on Do Not Disturb. The last thing she wanted was another interruption like before when her father tried to Facetime her repeatedly during one of her segments. When he couldn't get through her cell phone, he called the house phone. He could be relentless at times, especially if he was trying to be a doting father out of sheer guilt of not being there when they were younger. That debacle made her unplug the cordless house phone altogether. Before she could put her cell phone on Do Not Disturb, the phone rang. It was Dawn. Phyllis cringed as she swiped Red, sending her sister straight to voicemail.

"Sorry, baby sis. I only have 8 minutes until show time."

Right in the middle of her segment, she could not find her zester. She was live, there was no time to panic. "Hold on Food Fanatics, I think one of my daughters may have misplaced my lemon zester." *Shit! I just had to show off by using lemon zest as a garnishment. I was almost done with this segment.* She quickly exited the kitchen to yell up the stairs without hitting the pause button. She figured it would be a quick resolution, besides her viewers liked how she kept it "real" on her show, interruptions and all.

"Serena & Sabrina! Get down here right now!"

The sound of their little feet pattered down the stairs. Phyllis knew Sabrina be the first to round the corner because of her competitive nature. Sure enough, she was two steps ahead of Serena with an inquisitive expression on her face.

"Yes, mommy?" Serena said.

"Follow me, girls." Phyllis led them into the kitchen. She walked over to the utensil drawer, opened it slowly and pointed at an empty space. "Where is my lemon zester that was just sitting in this drawer on Tuesday?"

They both looked dumbfounded and didn't respond.

"So, did it grow legs and walk away?"

Serena shook her head. "No, but Sabrina used it to do our feet."

Sabrina nudged her sister on her arm and frowned.

Phyllis placed both hands on her hips. "To do your feet?"

"Yes, like when your do yours." Sabrina finally admitted.

"You mean like a pedicure?"

They nodded in unison.

Phyllis straightened her stance, bit her bottom lip trying to hold her laughter, but failed miserably. She bellowed out a laugh and Serena laughed with her. Sabrina furrowed her brows in confusion.

"My girls are too cute! Trying to be like mommy!" Phyllis continued laughing. "Can you do me a favor and get it for me so I can clean and soak it?"

"We can't." Sabrina confessed.

Phyllis titled her head and folded her arms across her chest. "Why not?"

Sabrina looked at her sister pointedly. Serena shot her eyes to the floor.

"Somebody better answer me in two seconds. One…two…" Phyllis always finished her one-two-count to strike fear in them and it usually worked.

"Because I spilled blue nail polish on it," Serena admitted.

Phyllis sighed.

"…And I finished painting it with red nail polish," Sabrina confessed again. "You know, like red, white and blue?"

Serena twisted the bottom of her t-shirt nervously while Sabrina stood with her back straight, unbothered.

"Oh, really?" Phyllis sighed. It wasn't that big of a deal, but she had to teach them a lesson, especially with the viewers watching this unfold. "Okay, hold out your hands." Phyllis smacked their hands as she usually did when they touched things that didn't belong to them and dismissed them.

She turned her attention to her viewers and noticed the numbers increased tremendously. A wide smile grew across her face. "Well, you all said that you wanted more interaction with my family. There you have it. Do you see what I have to go through around here? A lemon zester used for a pedicure! My twins are not only cute, but very creative!" She laughed nervously.

Phyllis finished her segment using the grater instead.

Chapter 12

"Oh, it's like that, huh?" Owen huffed.

He was coming for her, but Colette wasn't in the mood for it. Not today.

"Yep!" Colette responded confidently.

Owen folded his muscular arms across his chest. "You know damn well I can't have a house full of kids running wild when we got this newborn over here! He crying all day long as it is!"

It's a boy? Colette raised her eyebrows, but refused to give him the satisfaction of know her raw feelings about Owen having another son. So far, she had been the only woman to have his children and that, oddly enough, was enough to make her feel like she had the advantage over any woman who came along. Until now.

"Sounds like a personal problem to me."

"Wow!" Owen was at a loss for words for once. "I don't even know who you are right now. First, you turn into a church girl gone wild! Now you're just going completely wild abandoning your kids to have a free weekend. You ain't in your twenties anymore! What the hell you trying to be free from?"

"First of all, 'wild' is a bit of a stretch, Owen." Colette pointed her finger in his direction, which was thankfully across the room this time. "Second of all, it's none of your damn business about what I want to do nor who I want to do with *my* free time! If you sign these divorce papers you'll see language in here about a visitation schedule. That means that you will keep your children every other weekend."

"I heard all about you and that pastor," Owen replied as if he didn't hear a word she had just said about keeping his children. "What did you think he was gonna do, Colette? Whisk you and the kids away with him? Save you? Marry you? Why would he want you out of all the hoes in that church. It's some fine ass hoes up at that church, too!"

Colette grew silent and clenched her jaw repeatedly. What did she need to be embarrassed about anyway? She only gave love a second try just as he did. Had she known that Pastor Louis Paul was the bastard from her mother's past that caused her grief only to return to blackmail her out of her house, she would've never been involved romantically with him. Why couldn't anyone see that? Why couldn't her mother just tell her exactly who he was instead of trying to poison him? Why were things always so complicated in this family?

"It's no wilder than you knocking up your side piece!" she finally retorted. "You're the one almost fifty-years-old still having bastard babies with local hoes. Grow up and take care of *all* of your kids, Owen! I'll see you next week when I drop off *your* kids, you know, the ones that you know for sure belong to you!" Feeling vindicated from his sudden silence, she continued to dig the knife deeper. "And at least the pastor paid an attorney to draw up my divorce papers from you!"

Her thoughts replayed good times with Pastor – Big Louie – as she now referred to him since she knew exactly who he was. He was compassionate when it came to her circumstances with the children, allowing her to bring them to church office while she worked, making sure they were always fed, and all of her bills were paid. He was like a dream come true. Although he was controlling at times – much like Owen – she didn't mind so much because he was so good to her and the children.

Considering that he was a pastor, they never consummated their relationship – well, not the way she had hoped for anyway. Being a young bride restricted her from ever knowing any man except for Owen. He dominated their sex life; most times, she was not even a willing participant, but rather a lifeless, bottomless warm hole where he found pleasure from her pain. However, with the pastor she willingly participated in passionate kisses, petting and satisfying him orally even when he didn't initiate it. Although, he preferred her in complete submission, on her knees or wrists tied, she would eagerly comply with his demands. The pastor was a chunk of warm dark chocolate and much wider, but shorter than Owen's long, pointy penis that he nicknamed "The Punisher".

The last encounter with the pastor was on her knees with hands bound with rope. He guided her with his hand that clutched a chunk of her hair. He was so impressed by her oral skills that he gave her an early cash bonus and a Visa gift card of $500 for the children. Now, she was almost at the point of begging Owen for child support payments, but her pride wouldn't allow it. *Pride cometh before a fall,* she could hear Aunt Georgia chastising her. Maybe that was God's way of snapping her back to reality from her lustful thoughts.

Owen was cackling again. Colette waited patiently for him to finish. She snatched the divorce papers off the coffee table and held them out in his direction. He snorted while laughing this time around. When he finally finished, he straightened his back and a scowl spread across his face.

"I'm not going to sign those damn divorce papers. I never will either!

Colette exhaled a ball of fury. "For the love of God! *Why not?!*" "Because we were *never* married in the first place."

Chapter 13

"I'm sick of this poking and prodding. I'm sick of being cold in this damned hospital. I'm surprised that I don't have pneumonia by now. I've had just about enough of this foolishness. It's time for me to go home. They are messing with the wrong woman! They must not know who I am!"

One thing was for sure, nobody truly knew who Jonetta was nor what she was fully capable of doing. She had been through hell and back the majority of her life. Surviving is what she did best.

"It's time for me to get on with my life. I have to get back to my family. I'm so sure they are falling apart and needing me by now. Okay, wiggle your fingers and toes." Jonetta encouraged herself. *"Why is my arm so damn heavy and numb? The stroke. I had a damn stroke. Now I'm really pissed off. Wiggle your toes! Wiggle your toes!"*

Jonetta inhaled deeply and held her breath. *"Maybe the heart monitors will go off if I stop breathing."* She exhaled quickly. *"Bad idea. They'll only keep you in here longer if your heart stops, idiot! Wait a minute, I'm controlling my breathing. If I'm controlling that then that means…I'm fully awake. I'm not in a drug-induced coma! Come on, wiggle your fingers! Wiggle your toes!"*

Flexing her feet back and forth until she could bend her toes took more effort than she expected, but it was working. A slight sweat broke across her forehead and her hands began to get clammy. She felt it. She was definitely awake. A slight movement in her feet caused the sheets to move.*"That's it! You got it. Keep them moving. Any moment now, the nurse should be coming in here to poke. Wiggle your fingers! Open your eyes! Can you talk? Say something!"*

Her breathing labored, the heart monitor beeping increased with every movement she made. For the love of God, she couldn't figure out why her eyelids felt so heavy, but she blinked repeatedly until her eyes slightly opened. *"Why is it so dark? Oh my God! Am I blind? Why can't I see anything?"* She began to panic and tried to scream for help. It was a failed attempt. Her jaw felt like it had been glued shut. Imagine that. Jonetta Miller unable to talk?

A feeling of guilt swept over her. "*This is my punishment for attempting to kill Big Louie, but actually killing my sister instead. God, I swear that I live with lots of regret, but that one takes the cake. I have a lot of nerve asking any favors from you. So, as of today, I won't bother you anymore. I'm on my own. I got this."*

She painfully moved her jaw from right to left until she could slightly open her mouth.

"Make a sound. Any sound. Just let something come out of your mouth!" Jonetta tried to hum, but only a weak vibration escaped her mouth. *"That was pathetic!"* She shook her head. *"Oh my God! I just shook my head! I'm definitely awake!"* She turned her head towards the sounds in the hallway and saw a brighter light. *"I'm not blind! What the hell is this over my eyes?"* Her left arm felt like a brick. No, it felt like a dozen bricks were stacked on top of it. *Shit!* Instead, she concentrated on lifting her right arm. There was some movement, not much, but enough for her to flex her wrist. She moved each finger individually as if she were playing the piano. Again, her heart monitor increased its pace as she gained hope that her body would be hers once again. She was determined to get the hell out of there.

By now she felt a sweat break on her back, but she cleared her throat and tried again. “Help,” a whisper escaped her cottonmouth. *“Come on. You can do better than that!”* Just as she was about to try again she heard voices at her door. She instantly flexed her feet and moaned. Those were two things she knew for sure would grab their attention. The sweat forming underneath her breasts was irritating enough for her to want to snatch the sheets right off. *“God, if I only had the strength I’d leap from this bed. What the hell is taking them so long to get in here?”*

Jonetta cleared her throat again, louder this time.

“Mrs. Miller?”

“Ha! It worked!” Jonetta cleared her throat, moved her head to the right, and flexed her feet. That three-part combination gained her sight again. She squinted her eyes then opened them slowly to see an Asian male nurse staring at her, holding a lavender silk eye mask. *Nobody did that but Dawn,* Jonetta figured.

The male nurse immediately began to check her vitals, and then paged the doctor on call. “Welcome back, Mrs. Miller. My name is Niko.” He introduced himself as if Jonetta didn’t speak a lick of English.

Jonetta exhaled and tried to smile, but was unsuccessful.

“Don’t worry, once you begin physical therapy, you’ll feel like new money.” He walked over to her bedside and pressed a button to raise her to sit upright.

Jonetta groaned and shook her head. “Enough,” she said softly.

“Alright, alright. That’s as far as I will raise you,” Niko chuckled. “I just need to check your ears, take your blood pressure and call someone in your family. Oh, and call the doctor, too.”

Jonetta nodded and closed her eyes.

Back at the nurse’s station, Niko noticed a familiar face approaching and quickly hung up the desk phone. He nodded with approval, “You have impeccable timing. Your mother just woke up.”

Bishon stopped dead in his tracks. “What? Really?”

"Yeah, c'mon. I'll walk with you." Niko grabbed his pad and walked with Bishon. He noticed the change in his pace had slowed. "Are you good? Need a minute?"

Bishon cleared his throat. "No, I'm okay. I just wasn't expecting to be the first person she sees… you know… considering I was the last person she saw when…" His voice trailed off as his thoughts forced flashbacks of Jonetta hitting the ground in the parking lot when let her know that she was his mother. Finally, a void had been filled in his life and in an instant, it led to tragedy.

"Actually, I was the first person she saw." Niko chuckled as he lingered at the doorway to Jonetta's room before opening the door. He eyed Bishon carefully and could tell that he was nervous. "Listen, your mother might be a little groggy, slow to speak even. We still need to run tests and check her mobility skills, but the good news is she's awake."

"Have you called anyone in the family yet?"

"I was just about to do that, but then I saw you coming down the hallway. So, I can leave that task to you now." Niko patted him on the shoulder, flashed a smile, knocked on the door twice with his knuckles and opened it.

A gush of cold air greeted them with the sounds of the machines beeping and whizzing. Jonetta was partly sitting up with her eyes closed.

"Mrs. Miller, look who I found." Niko approached her bedside, immediately putting his stethoscope buds in his ears. He was about to place the diaphragm on her chest until she began coughing. "You don't want me touching you at all, huh? That's okay, Mrs. Miller. Get it all out. I'll be back soon anyway. Your son is here."

Jonetta opened her eyes, slowly turned her head to get a good look at Bishon and began to moan.

Bishon rushed to her side and grabbed her hand. He smoothed her wiry grey hair and searched her face with worry.

"What's wrong with her? Can she talk?"

"Yes, she can. I think she's just overwhelmed and happy to see you," Niko explained. "Take all the time you need. The doctor will be making his rounds shortly."

Bishon pulled up a chair and took a seat before his knees buckled. The last time they were alone together, she ended up in the hospital. He had tried to explain to everyone what happened, what he found out, why he was at the funeral, and why Jonetta passed out. Everything and everyone was chaotic that nobody paid him any attention. Now, they would not have a choice but to pay him attention, to accept him in the family.

"Son," Jonetta said finally. Her voice sounded dead, even to her own ears.

Bishon squeezed her hand. "I don't know what to say… I'm so sorry that I … No, I'm not sorry that I found out that you're my mother. I'm sorry that I told you at your sister's funeral. I'm sorry that I didn't use wisdom. I was just so excited and nervous. I'm so sorry that my news sent you over the edge. I'm just so sorry that this stroke happened to you."

Jonetta squeezed his hand and shook her head. "I'm happy."

"Mrs. Miller… ummm… I mean… well, I actually don't know what to call you," he exhaled sharply with frustration.

"Mom."

Bishon shook his head and sighed heavily. "That won't work. I already have a mom, and she's not been herself since all of this happened. It's so much we need to sort through. But, I'm so glad to know that you're my birth mother. Please know that. We'll figure it out."

He babbled nervously, wishing someone could intervene on his behalf. No such luck. It was just the two of them for now, until the others arrived.

"Oh! Who would you like me to call first?" he searched his pants pocket for his mobile phone. He pulled it out and began to search his contact list. "They'll all be so happy that you're awake. They would fly here if they could. So just tell me who to call first."

Bishon stopped scrolling and stared into Jonetta's eyes. They had the same shaped eyes. He slowly examined her whole face from her ears, to chin, to forehead, to cheekbone structure. They definitely had the same shaped head and similar features. Funny, he had never noticed any of their similarities before. Why would he? He held his hand next to hers and compared skin tones; his was darker. *Who is my real father?* He pushed that question out of his mind. One day at a time. Everything would be revealed eventually. Right now, he had the pleasure of knowing his birth mother was in his life all along.

"You're my beautiful son. You're mine."

Chapter 14

It was around twelve thirty in the afternoon when Norman was disrupted from his normal routine. He was just about to sit down to catch up on the last three episodes of *The Black List* when he heard the loud banging on his front door.

"Dad! Open up!" Colette frantically banged on the door with the side of her fist. She adjusted the baby on her hip and rang the doorbell repeatedly. Finally, her father snatched open the door.

"For the love of God, Colette! Where's the fire?"

Colette barged into her father's house, dropped the diaper bag on the floor in the foyer and plopped the baby on the carpet a few feet away barely in the living room. Tears fell from her eyes and she flicked them away just as quickly as they fell. She tried her best to form a sentence, but her shallow breathing wouldn't allow it.

Norman grabbed her by her shoulders to calm her. "How did you get here? What's going on?"

"I… I…took an Uber," Colette answered with a knot in her throat.

"Is it your mother? Did something happen to my Netta?" Norman reached in his pocket to check his cell phone for a missed call. When he saw none, he searched his daughter's face for answers.

"No, it's not Mama!" she blurted out through sobs.

He exhaled and glanced at Delilah, who was crawling around on the carpet, content. It was probably the norm for her to be on the floor, but Norman didn't like it one bit. "Where are the other children?"

"At school."

"Oh, right." Norman grew impatient. "Well, tell me what's going on. You come over here banging on my door and ringing the bell like it was a major emergency. So where's the fire? Spit it out!"

Colette whimpered, covering her mouth. "He said… he said…that," she gagged, trying to repeat the awful truth that she had just learned.

"Who? Who said what?"

"Owen!" she said with her bottom lip quivering.

"Oh," Norman grunted. "What did he say to you now?"

Colette shook her head in disbelief and mashed her lips. She didn't want to repeat the ugly truth. That revelation meant that everything that she knew about her life was a big lie.

Delilah shrieked and Colette dashed into the living room where she found her baby ripping out pages from a magazine.

"Those are your grandma's magazines," Norman wagged his finger at his granddaughter. He picked her up and planted a kiss on her cheek.

Colette reached for her baby, but Norman pointed to the sofa instead.

"You just have a seat. I've got my grandbaby," he said, getting comfortable in his chair. "Now, tell me what Owen said to get you so upset like this."

The tears had begun to dry up on her cheeks until she tried to speak again about their conversation. "I'm sorry, Dad. I just can't stop crying."

Norman sat back and waited patiently.

Colette composed herself and began, "Owen came by the house. I just wanted him to sign the divorce papers." Her chest heaved and a loud sob escaped.

"Did he hit you again?" Norman asked, leaning forward and shifting Delilah on his knees.

Colette shook her head. "That probably would've been a softer blow."

"What?!" Norman shrieked in disbelief.

"Dad, he told me that he would never sign the divorce papers because… because… we were never married in the first place!" Colette threw herself across the sofa and cried into the cushions.

Norman exhaled and rocked Delilah back and forth, although it was Colette who needed comforting. He allowed a few moments to pass before he expressed his thoughts.

"Well, seems to me that should be a relief to you, baby."

"How?" Colette asked. She sat up, wiped her nose with her sleeve.

"Now you don't have to pressure nor beg him to sign any divorce papers. Big Louie shelled out money to a divorce lawyer for no reason at all! Hell, that's his loss too! Not yours. See? They are the losers. You came out winning, sweetie!"

"Nooooo!" Colette disputed. "I feel like a loser. I've been tricked by Owen! I've been committing fornication all these years! I feel like a damn fool, Dad!"

"Fornication? Colette, the God that I know is not going to send you to hell over another person's sin. So just calm down." Norman sighed. *There is no getting through to you today.* "But tell me this, second daughter of mine, how on Earth did you not know that you were never legally married to this man all these years?" Colette was about to explain her reasoning until the doorbell rang. The pounding on the door startled them both. It was followed by ringing again.

"Who the hell is this at my door banging like a fool?" Norman passed Delilah to Colette and shot to his feet. "Hold on, Colette. I'll be right back."

The knocks on the door became louder as he approached. He peered out the side window panel. It was Dawn. The moment he opened the door, she rushed right past him crying uncontrollably.

"Dawn! Sweetheart, calm down. What's wrong?" Norman closed the door behind him and embraced his youngest daughter.

Colette appeared in the foyer, holding Delilah. "What happened to you? What's going on?"

"Bishon just told me that… he's my … he's *our* brother." Dawn said out loud for the first time. "Mama has a son."

"When did you find out?" Norman asked somberly, closing the door softly. *This is just not my day,* he thought.

"Dad, you *knew*?" Dawn asked in disbelief. Disappointment spread across her face like wild fire as more tears welled in her eyes.

Norman placed his hands on Dawn's hunched shoulders and replied softly, "Listen, there just wasn't a good time to discuss something like that…"

"Dad! How could you *not* tell us? How is this even possible? Does Mama know that her son is alive?" Colette blurted out questions.

Norman nodded his head. "Yes, and we believe that's what caused her stroke. It was shocking news to me, too. It's taking time for me to process all of this while your mother is still in the hospital."

"Who is 'we'?" Colette asked.

"Let's all sit down and take some deep breaths." He suggested as they walked into the living room.

Dawn chose a cushion on the sofa furthest away from her father. Disgust, disappointment and betrayal were all toiling in the pit of her stomach. She patiently allowed her father to explain what he knew and how he knew, but it only caused vomit to rise in her throat. Waiting for the moment to hear her father say, "It isn't true. This man is insane." never happened. It was true. It was real. This was happening to her.

"Excuse me!" Dawn rushed to the guest bathroom, slammed the door and dove for the toilet. Chunks of breakfast splattered into to the bowl then onto her face. None of that mattered as much as who she had allowed inside of her body, and what was growing inside of her at this very moment.

After a few minutes passed, Colette went to check on her baby sister. She heard the bathroom water running and Dawn crying softly.

"May I come in?" Colette asked turning the doorknob. She peeked in to find Dawn curled up on the floor like a lost child crying for her mother. "Oh, no. Come on, Dawn, get off the floor." Colette extended her hand to help her sister, but she refused.

"You don't understand *just* how bad this is," Dawn said, wiping her nose.

Colette took a seat on top of the toilet lid. "Listen, we'll have to work through all of this as a family. This is some deep stuff to understand, especially if Mama thought her son was stillborn all these years. We just need to get together and talk about everything," Colette sighed, allowing her own words to sink in for a moment. "Now this all makes sense why Mama had a stroke. That's a lot for a person to hear on the day of her sister's funeral. Bishon should've known better than that."

"That's not even the half of it. I'm sure it was a combination of everything that caused Mama to have a stroke," Dawn replied mindlessly twirling her hair. "This is worse than a soap opera and reality show combined. This is all my fault and I feel terrible. I just don't know what to do!"

"You don't know what to do about what? If you ask me, it's Bishon's fault for opening his big mouth at the funeral. How is this your fault, Dawn?" Colette asked desperately wanting to know.

"I'm pregnant," she confessed, covering her face in shame.

Colette gasped. Before she had a chance to respond, Norman was hollering down the hallway. She quickly opened the bathroom door to listen closely.

"Dad, what did you say?" Colette asked.

"I said...Let's go! Your mother is awake!"

Chapter 15

"She's awake," Barbara announced gravely when she ended her phone call with Bishon. She gripped the phone so tight that the whites of her knuckles began to show.

"Sweetheart," Stanton reached for her hands, easing the phone from her grasp. "Let's just see how this goes. We have to support Bishon, no matter what."

"We should've never encouraged him to find his birth mother," Barbara admitted regretfully. The very thought of Bishon seeking love from another woman and calling her "mom" made Barbara very envious. *He's my son!*

"Let me make you some tea," Stanton offered. He pulled a lemon from the refrigerator and grabbed a can of herbal loose leaf tea from the pantry.

"I don't want any tea!" Barbara hissed.

"Okay, then. I'll make myself some tea," Stanton replied calmly. Once she smelled the sweet aroma, he knew that she'd want some hibiscus lemon tea.

"I want my life back the way it was. She doesn't deserve him in her life now! I raised that boy! Jonetta clearly *never* wanted him!"

Stanton cringed. "That might not be the truth, sweetheart."

"Why else would he end up on the steps of a church?"

"Norman told me that Jonetta believed that her son was dead all these years."

"Dead?"

Stanton nodded and continued, "Long story-short, Jonetta had fallen down the basement steps, which caused her to go into early labor. Her great-aunts called one of their doctors, he gave her meds to knock her out. It was a difficult delivery. After she woke up, Jonetta's great-aunts told her that her baby died since he was premature and all. Apparently, it was one of them who dropped him off at the church, not Jonetta."

Barbara slumped down in the chair and glided her hand across the cold marble table. Her hands, always well-manicured, were aged with a few earned wrinkles. She prided herself on being stylish and classy, remaining the calm in the midst of many storms they faced during their marriage. Even though, at this moment in time, she would be well within her right to be in a fit of rage, all the ill feelings she had about the ordeal seemed to slowly dissipate. That was a horrible thing to do to anybody. *What type of evil people were they?* She couldn't imagine believing that a loved one was dead for over forty-years only to find out they were alive and well.

Barbara sighed and sat upright. "Well, at least we know the family. Even though Jonetta doesn't seem like a woman who has many friends, I'd be willing to share our role as mothers and even grandmothers… if it comes to that."

Stanton grunted. "Dawn being pregnant by her half-brother is what is most terrifying and disgusting to me!"

"Do we know for sure that it's Bishon's baby?"

Stanton frowned as he pondered another possible father. "In this case, I hope to God that he's *not* the father!"

"My goodness!" Barbara exclaimed. "Listen to us! We've been reduced to a reality television show! A long-lost son, a daughter having sex with her half-brother, a baby on the way and nobody knows who the father could be! Somebody call Maury Povich and Jerry Springer!"

Stanton finally took a seat at the table with his wife and held her hand. He hadn't shared his private fear that Jonetta would take complete control of being the number one mother in his life and grandmother since it was *her* daughter that was pregnant. She had three daughters, no son – that she knew of – until now. Jonetta didn't have a "take the backseat" type of personality at all. She was about to be in her glory with Bishon.

If Stanton had known that encouraging Bishon to find his birth mother would spin into a tangled web, he would've kept his mouth shut.

"Sweetheart, I'll own some of the blame for all of this," Stanton admitted as he put cobalt blue kettle on the stove.

Barbara squinted her eyes. "What do you mean by that?"

Stanton cleared his throat and continued, "I believe a tip that I gave Bishon led him to Jonetta. I shared with our son that the loose women in *that* house who got pregnant would drop off their babies at churches nearby. They weren't allowed to keep the babies if they planned on still 'working' there… if you get my drift."

"How would you know that?" she demanded.

Stanton squared his shoulders and looked his wife in the eyes, "Listen, Barbara, I've been in this community a long time. I know a lot of things, seen a lot of things, ya know? The fact of the matter is, Bishon found Jonetta, his birth mother, and now she's awake. So let's take it from here and be supportive."

Barbara sat in silence and considered everything they had just discussed. Every avenue her mind wandered down led to a lose-win outcome, with her being the biggest loser. But now was not the time to be selfish, she had to consider what her son was up against.

"I think we should head over to the hospital to be with Bishon."

Chapter 16

On their way to the hospital, Colette requested to stop by the school to pick up the children for an early dismissal. Against his better judgment, Norman obliged. This was not a time for ruckus in the hospital lobby. His heart was anxious to see the love of his life and to find out exactly what condition she was in. *God, I hope that I'll be able to care for her the way she needs.*

While the children piled in his car, Dawn called Phyllis to meet them at the hospital, but there was no answer.

"Dad, slow down," Dawn said, reaching for his hand. It was gripped so tight on the wheel that his skin looked smooth. "Phyllis didn't answer. She might be…"

"Try her again," Norman insisted.

"Dad, I called three times. It's going straight to voicemail," Dawn replied frustrated, tossing her phone inside of her purse.

"I sent her a text message. She'll see it, Dad. Don't worry," Colette chimed in from the backseat.

"Well, you know how you girls are if you're the last to find out something. It's like a competition or something."

Dawn smirked. Her father was right, they hated not being in the loop on family information. If one sister found out information before the other they needed explanations as to why they were the last to know.

"I want everyone at the hospital to see your Mama," Norman continued. "This is a crucial time for all of us. We'll have to devise a plan once I get her home."

"Grandma's coming home?" Cornell asked, leaning up to the front of the car so he could see his grandfather's face.

"Sit back, Cornell," Colette scolded. She put her finger to her lip and shook her head. "It's quiet time right now."

"We have quiet time in the car, too?" Lydia asked.

"Yes, it's whenever I say it is, like now. Shhhh!" Colette instructed. She looked down at Delilah who was nodding off for a nap. *Good!* Colette thought. One less child to tussle with once they arrived.

Once they arrived at the hospital, Norman didn't waste any time seeking out familiar faces at the nurses' station. He wanted answers. He was so focused that he walked right past Bishon who had been perched in a corner like a child on punishment.

"Hey," Bishon spoke to Dawn, stood to greet her and almost gave her a hug.

She flinched as he approached her. "Hi," she responded softly.

"Hi, I'm Colette," she shook his hand.

Bishon nodded and cleared his throat. "Yeah, I figured. Nice to meet you."

"Well, this is awkward!" Dawn remarked and took a seat. Colette settled in the waiting room with the children who were firing a dozen questions all at once.

"Maybe you should call Owen to come pick them up?" Dawn suggested as kindly as she could.

Colette shot her a disapproving look. The mere mention of their father would spark a totally different conversation. One she was not prepared to have at the moment in front of 'company'.

"Can we go with Daddy today?" Ruthie asked.

Colette shot daggers towards Dawn.

Dawn shrugged and mouthed, *"My bad!"*

"Let's just say a quick prayer for grandma, okay?" Colette redirected the conversation. "Come on, Dawn, let's pray."

Before Dawn could bow her head in prayer, out the corner of her eye, she could have sworn that she saw Raffi down the hallway. The guy had the same stature, hair was long and locked like his, but she wasn't quite sure. When she tried to get a better look, Colette had begun the prayer.

Immediately after they said Amen, the doctor appeared with Norman by his side.

"Girls, listen up. The doc has some news for us," Norman announced. "Oh, hi Bishon."

"Mr. Miller," Bishon nodded.

Was that him? Why would he be on this floor? That's all I need is both of these men here at the same time. Wait. Oh my God! Is Chena alright? Is that why he's here? But this isn't her floor for chemo therapy. Dawn's mind raced as she tried to listen to the doctor's update and instructions about her mother. She heard the most important words spoken: "stroke, therapy, right side, recovery, going home", but that was about it.

A vibration from her phone distracted her even further from the being in the moment. It was a text from Bishon who was standing five feet away from her.

Bishon: We need to talk after we leave. Just me and you.

Dawn: Ok...

When she glanced up from the phone, her eyes met his, but he quickly looked away. *Damn, this is deep! He can't even look at me.*

"I'm gonna see your Mama first," Norman announced and disappeared down the hall with the nurse. It wasn't up for debate. He was going back there alone until he determined that she was good for company. He didn't know what to expect. He had known a few coworkers who suffered from having a stroke and they were never quite the same with their speech, movements nor facial expressions. Prayers were being sent up as he stiffly walked towards Jonetta's room.

The elevator dinged and Phyllis rushed towards her family with the twins in tow before the doors could completely open.

"I got here soon as I could! I had a food segment to do today on Facebook Live," Phyllis explained as she guided Serena and Sabrina to available chairs in the lobby. "Sit here with your cousins and no fighting. Do you understand me?"

They replied simultaneously, "Yes, mommy."

Dawn hugged Phyllis warmly. She was relieved that she received their missed calls and text messages. Colette joined them with Delilah clutched to her neck and they all embraced one another.

"We gotta be strong for Dad," Phyllis whispered in their huddle. They agreed and broke their embrace.

"How's Mama doing?" Phyllis asked as she took Delilah into her arms and bounced her on her hip.

Dawn and Colette brought her up to speed about their mother's condition, Colette and Owen never being married, Dawn's pregnancy dilemma, and most importantly Bishon being their half-brother.

"Our brother?" Phyllis eyed Bishon carefully. She could see the resemblance to their mother in his features, but not his complexion. Jonetta was much more fair-skinned than Bishon. *He must look exactly like his rapist of a father.*

"Yes, we're related," Dawn replied grimly.

"Wait a second, Phyllis. So, you knew that Dawn was pregnant and didn't mention it to me?" Colette asked frowning.

"It wasn't *my* business to tell," Phyllis hissed.

"Now is not the time for that petty shit, Colette!" Dawn scolded her sister. "Didn't Dad just mention in the car how we need to stop that foolishness and grow up a bit?"

They agreed unanimously.

"Where is Dad, anyway?" Phyllis asked.

"He's back there with Mama now," Dawn responded.

"Well, it seems like a good time to have a little family reunion conversation with our new brother." Phyllis said as she passed Delilah back to Colette and marched towards Bishon who was sitting quietly in a corner by the window.

Dawn tried to stop her, but it was too late.

Bishon sat upright when he saw Phyllis approaching.

"Hi, Phyllis. Remember me?" Bishon flashed an awkward smile.

Phyllis sat down beside him and exhaled sharply. "I surely do remember the day you came to the family house. You were mighty persistent," she remembered with a chuckle. "Now I understand why you grabbed my arm and demanded answers."

"Sorry about that," Bishon said, gently touching her hand.

Phyllis flicked her wrist, "No worries. I just want to know what your next steps are in our family."

"I'm not sure that I'm following."

"It's bad enough that I'm not the oldest anymore and that our mother is recovering from a stroke, thanks to *your* news. We have yet to fully vet to see if it's even true. And if that's not enough of a headache, you and Dawn have quite the dilemma on your hands with a baby on the way. There's going to be quite a few feathers ruffled while decisions are made and D.N.A. test results come back. So, if there's anything else up your sleeve, maybe you should run it past me first."

Bishon was baffled and didn't quite know how to respond to her jabs and accusations. "D.N.A tests? Who needs to take a test?"

"You do! We need to know for sure that you're our mother's son."

"I don't need to do a damn thing!" Bishon stood to his feet and continued, "Furthermore, I don't have anything up my sleeve and I really don't appreciate your insinuations."

Phyllis raised her eyebrows, "Is that right?"

"That is *my* mother laying back there right now, too! We had already formed a friendship once she came to work at my dental office, remember? I was the only one here when she just woke up. Sorry to disappoint you, but *our* mother is very happy to see me. She knows that I am her son that she believed was dead for over forty years! I'm not going anywhere!" Bishon walked away furious.

Dawn watched the whole conversation unfold and now he was headed her way. *Oh shit!* She held her breath.

"Let's talk, now!" Bishon demanded and grabbed Dawn by the hand.

Barbara walked off the elevator before Stanton and marched towards the nurse's station bypassing the family. Stanton was about to call out to her, but he thought better of it. She was in a nasty mood and probably would make a scene. An unforgivable one, especially at a time like this. Instead he spoke to Colette and Phyllis in order to distract them from his wife's misstep.

"I'm sorry ma'am, but unless you're family, we cannot release any information." The nurse informed Barbara. She knew that, of course, but her interests were more about the condition of her competition. *If Jonetta was unable to speak, then that would be even better.*

"Sweetheart," Stanton called out to Barbara, waving her over to him. "This is Phyllis, Colette, and their children."

"I know who they are!" Barbara snapped. "How's your mother doing?"

"She's awake and talking," Colette replied.

Barbara grimaced, but then quickly flashed a tight smile. *That's just my luck.*

"Mama had a mild stroke, thank God. She will need physical therapy on her right side just to regain her strength. That's all we really know for now," Phyllis added.

"In case you were wondering, we're here for Bishon's sake. You simply cannot imagine the anguish and turmoil happening inside of him," Barbara remarked.

"And…we're here to support Norman, of course. He's my friend," Stanton added with a nod.

Phyllis nodded in return. "I'm sure he'll appreciate it."

"Hey! Cut it out!" Colette marched towards the children. They became antsy, fussing over which YouTube video they were going to watch next while sharing one tablet between the five of them.

"They are probably tired and need a nap," Barbara remarked.

"We're not going anywhere until we see our mother," Phyllis countered.

"Have you seen *my* son?" Barbara retorted.

Stanton glanced around the corner where he saw Bishon and Dawn having an intense conversation.

Phyllis raised her eyebrows. For some inexplicable reason she became defensive. *That's my mother's son!*

"*Your* son?" Phyllis questioned.

"Sweetheart, why don't we take a seat for now?" He guided her to a chair nearby and shot her a look that read: *Now is not the time for being petty.* "What's gotten into you? We're here for Bishon, remember?"

Barbara took a seat, looked straight ahead and clutched her purse closely to her chest. In her own right, she was hurting and feeling insecure about losing Bishon as a son. Her life was about to take an unexpected turn and she wanted everyone to know that she wasn't going anywhere. No matter what, Bishon Franklyn was her son and she would battle anyone who claimed any different.

"Dawn, look, this is…"

"Fucked up?"

Bishon nodded. "I'm sorry."

"For what?"

"I didn't know you were my half-sister. I was devastated when I found out because… I was totally into you, wanting you… Dawn, you were *it* for me. There was no other woman for me. So, if you were pregnant and we weren't in this situation, then I'd be overjoyed about you having my baby," Bishon lamented.

Dawn folded her arms and remarked, "Really?"

"Yes, I would!" Bishon continued, "But since you're my half-sister, you cannot have this baby."

"Who are you to tell me what to do with *my* body?"

Dawn was right, he had a lot of nerve telling her what to do. He didn't share his private fear that the baby would probably have all types of defects and learning disabilities due to their direct bloodline, not to mention the questions the child would have and the teasing it would endure from other children once the truth was leaked about the parents.

"Listen, all I'm saying is if we hadn't rushed this thing… we would not be in this predicament."

"*You* are not in any predicament!" Dawn corrected him adamantly. "We slept together, big deal! We can move past that issue. Plenty of people make the mistake of sleeping with someone, then regret it."

"Yeah, but I doubt it's with a sibling!"

Dawn shrugged. *Well, that's the damn truth.* "Regardless, the biggest issue for me, right now, is that I am pregnant. Honestly, you may not be the father, so you can stop stressing."

Bishon's expression changed. He leaned against the wall, rubbed his beard in thought and replied, "Wow!"

"Yeah, it's like that. You were not the only man that I was seeing," Dawn admitted. "So, you just might be off the hook."

Norman appeared in the waiting area looking exhausted.

"How's Mama doing?" Colette asked.

"Can we see Mama now?" Phyllis asked hopeful.
"She's only asking for Bishon."

Chapter 17

Phyllis ran down the corridor before Bishon could make a move. In the distance, she heard her name being called by her family, but there was no stopping her. Bishon had done enough already. It was her turn to see her mother.

"Mama," Phyllis panted. She stood a few feet away from her mother while she caught her breath. "Mama, are you awake?"

Jonetta turned her head towards the doorway and extended her left hand. Phyllis hurried to her side with tears welling in her eyes and clasped her hands around her mother's. The tears spilled down her cheeks, staining the sheets. "Mama, I've been so worried about you. I've been praying for you. I'm so glad you're awake. You just never know how much a person means to you until… well, I'm just so glad that you're awake, Mama."

Jonetta squeezed her hand as firmly as she could and let out a moan.

Phyllis buried her head on her mother's shoulder for a moment, then lifted her head and wiped her tears with her sleeve. *Pull it together, girl!* She pulled up a chair and took a seat. "Can you talk? Do you need some water? Do you want to sit up? Tell me what you need, Mama."

Jonetta shook her head. "No, I need a mirror."

Phyllis let out a chuckle and searched through her purse for a pocket mirror. "You know I have one, Mama." Phyllis flashed a huge smile once she found it and handed it to her mother. "Here you go, Mama. Let me help you get yourself together."

When Jonetta didn't reach for the mirror Phyllis immediately apologized. "I forgot that fast, I'm sorry, Mama."

"I need your help," Jonetta said softly. This was a new predicament for her. Usually, she was self-sufficient and didn't require much assistance from anyone.

"I got you, Mama. Don't worry, with physical therapy, you'll be your old self again," Phyllis said. She angled the mirror to the best of her ability so her mother could get a full view of her face.

Jonetta smacked the mirror away and clenched her eyes shut once she got a good look at herself. "Put it away!"

Phyllis gasped. *Well, damn! Your old self is coming back quicker than I expected.* "Mama, I can help you look presentable. Just let me smooth your hair down and…"

"No!" Jonetta replied fiercely, shaking her head. "I feel like I've been beat up and I look like it, too! Get me out of here. I want to go home…today."

Phyllis exhaled sharply. There was nothing she could do about that. "Mama, the doctor said they are keeping you until tomorrow. You'll be released late afternoon, early evening at the latest. So don't go working yourself up. You don't want to give them any excuse to keep you longer. Do you?"

Jonetta knew that was the case, but she wanted to leave today. She wanted to be at home, in peace with Bishon. He was the last face she saw before she hit the ground and he was the first face she saw when she came to. She knew for a fact that was nothing but God. Now she just wanted to go home to spend all of her time with him.

"Where is my son?"

"Mama, let's just take one thing at a time, okay?" Phyllis replied, squeezing her hand. "We don't know for a fact that he's your son."

Jonetta snatched her hand away and glared at Phyllis. "Bishon is my son! I know it in my soul."

"Do you really believe that your aunts would be so cruel to tell you that your son died at birth?"

"Yes!" Jonetta replied incredulously. "If you only knew just how evil they were and the things they made me do just to have a roof over my head and food in my stomach, trust me, you would never question this situation."

Phyllis sat back in the chair and contemplated Bishon actually being her half-brother and what it meant for all of them, especially Dawn. "I'm only hoping he's not your son… for Dawn's sake."

Jonetta turned her head away. She didn't want to think about that right now. She just wanted to have joy in this moment. Having a mild stroke was the last thing she needed to do at a time like this. But with all the regret, grief and overwhelming guilt she felt at her sister's funeral the news Bishon shared was just too much. It didn't upset her, quite the contrary, she was delighted and excited, but it was just too much all at once.

"Just go get my son."

The nurses rolled food carts down the hallway and the aromas reminded Dawn that she was hungry. "I need to get something to eat before I vomit or faint." She announced to no one in particular.

"I'll go with you," Bishon offered.

"No!" Dawn contested.

"Y'all leaving me and Colette with all the kids?" Norman asked in disbelief. He reached for Delilah who was getting squirmy on her mother's lap. "I'm sure these big kids are getting hungry, too."

"I'm super hungry," Cornell said, patting his stomach.

"You're always hungry," Colette countered and rolled her eyes.

"The lunch at school was disgusting! Dad said I'm a growing boy and I should eat like…" Cornell took a moment to count on his fingers, "Six times a day. I only ate twice today, mom."

"Is that what he said?" Colette grimaced. The very mention of Owen made her sick to her stomach.

Dawn shook her head at their banter. *I'm definitely not in the mood.* "Dad, I just need some alone time right now," Dawn explained. "I need to clear my head. I'll be back."

Bishon was tempted to follow her to the elevator despite her wishes, but thought better of it. He took a seat near his parents with a disgusted look on his face.

"Son, we will get through this together," Barbara reassured him, patting his knee.

He nodded and excused himself. "I need to make some calls to the office. I'll be back."

"Stanton, thanks so much for coming," Norman said as he finally took a seat.

"Don't mention it, man. This involves all of us. We just wanted to show support," Stanton explained. "Bishon is really upset and confused…"

"Confused about what?" Norman asked.

Stanton rubbed his beard thoughtfully before responding. The last thing he wanted to do was offend anyone, especially his overly sensitive wife. "He just wants to do the right thing."

Barbara shifted in her seat and searched her husband's face. She didn't know what he meant by that and right now she wasn't going to ask any questions.

"Well, Dawn and Bishon are grown. It doesn't matter what we advise them to do in this sticky situation. They will need to make the decisions and live with them," Norman replied.

"Yes, but whatever they decide will affect all of our lives, forever," Barbara replied resolutely.

"That's true, Dad," Colette chimed in. "Bishon is still our half-brother and there's no changing that. Whether or not they have the baby will still cause a ripple effect."

"Aunty Dawn is having a baby?" Cornell asked.

"We're having a baby cousin?" Lydia asked, perking up.

"Stay out of grown folk's conversation!" Barbara hissed.

"Hey! Don't talk to my children like that!" Colette snapped.

"I suggested that you take these children home a while ago, but you wouldn't listen to that good advice. Now they are listening to details of this dysfunctional family drama that they don't need to hear!" Barbara countered.

"Dysfunctional?" Norman retorted. "Now hold on, Barbara…"

"Sweetheart, let's get some air," Stanton suggested. He stood to his feet and helped his wife to hers before things got ugly.

"I think that's a good idea," Colette said, eyeing Barbara up and down.

Colette shook her head and handed her mobile phone and ear buds to Cornell as a distraction. "Here you go, son. Pull up a movie or game and share an ear bud with your sister."

"I want to be right here after Bishon talks to Jonetta," Barbara insisted. "There's no telling what will take place on the set of this reality show."

"You know what…I'm gonna pray for you!" Colette retorted.

"We're all going to need prayer!" Barbara remarked over her shoulder as Stanton pulled her away.

Norman and Colette exchanged glances of exhaustion and disgust.

After planting a kiss on her mother's cheek and leaving the room, Phyllis walked towards the nurse's station with a coy expression on her face and mumbled something. *I'll fix this fiasco.* As she waltz towards the family, Bishon reemerged to her delight. He was just in time to hear her announcement, "Mama needs her rest and doesn't want anymore visitors."

Chapter 18

"We need to take turns helping Dad out with Mama." Phyllis began the conversation. She had invited Colette to stop by while her oldest three were visiting Owen. They needed to discuss a plan on helping Jonetta with therapy and helping their father around the house.

"True. We need to work out a schedule since our lives are all pretty busy right up through here," Dawn replied, stuffing tortilla chips with salsa in her mouth.

"You do realize that none of us have a job, right?" Colette remarked, giving a side eye.

"Well, that's going to change for me really soon," Phyllis replied as a smile crept across her face.

Dawn repositioned herself on the sofa. "Is that right? Damien should be thrilled."

"What about daycare for the twins?" Colette asked. She glanced at Delilah who was sound asleep on the opposite sofa.

Phyllis held up her hands. "Pause a moment and let me share my news with you. Based on viewership, likes and comments, I have been contacted by a Facebook representative to conduct my own live cooking show!"

"Oh, my goodness! That is a great opportunity!" Dawn exclaimed, beaming with pride. "You know I'll have to do a special guest appearance, right?"

Phyllis laughed.

"Where will the twins be while you film?"

"Right there in the house. Sometimes, I'll put them on camera, too. The audience loves the twins. So you see? No need for daycare because I won't have to leave my house at all. I will have a camera crew once a week come into our home to film while I make delicious recipes." Phyllis sat back with a huge smile on her face, pleased with herself.

"And what does Damien think about all of this?" Colette asked.

"I haven't told him yet," Phyllis responded munching on tortillas.

"What!?" Dawn and Colette replied.

"It's been a lot going on lately. I'll tell him this week, but I know for a fact that he probably won't like the idea of strangers in the house," Phyllis explained and shrugged her shoulders.

"Husbands!" Dawn remarked.

"Tell me about it. I still have a huge issue on my hands with that damn Owen," Colette said fiercely.

"Well, thankfully, he's *not* your husband," Dawn replied and giggled.

"Yeah, I'm with Dad and Dawn on this one. Count your blessings and be grateful that you were never married to that asshole!" Phyllis said adamantly.

"But what about spousal support? I had all of that language drawn up in the divorce papers."

"Just go to child support court," Dawn commented, waving her off. "That's what all the baby mamas do."

"I'm not a baby mama!" Colette replied fiercely.

Dawn and Phyllis chuckled.

"Speaking of which, I certainly don't wanna be nobody's baby mama," Dawn admitted. "That's why I'm having an abortion."

"An abortion?" Colette gasped. "No! Don't kill your baby!"

Dawn shook her head and rolled her eyes. "Look who's talking! What happened with your last pregnancy?"

"I tripped and fell down the stairs," Colette said avoiding eye contact.

Dawn rolled her eyes. "I was not looking for your approval. Not everyone wants to be 'Fertile Myrtle' like you, having kids running around wild. I've made up my mind. It's the only way out."

"Don't do this. You don't even know whose baby it is," Colette pleaded desperately. She looked to Phyllis to back her up and chime in.

"That's true," Phyllis said, nodding. "But it's Dawn's body. It's her decision. The way these abortion laws are changing, she better act fast before Illinois jumps on the Handmaid's Tale bandwagon!"

"Thank you very much," Dawn nodded.

"Also, the fact that it could be Bishon's baby… well…there's way too many health risks and birth defects to consider, since he's our brother."

"*Half*-brother," Colette reminded her.

Phyllis nodded in agreement. "That part."

"It's a lose-lose situation either way," Dawn admitted. "I'm not trying to be tied to Raffi nor Bishon for the rest of my life either way. For God's sake, I'm certainly not trying to have a retarded baby either."

A moment of silence passed as they all considered the possible outcomes.

"Do you know what this makes me?" Dawn asked.

Her sisters exchanged glances, looking baffled.

"What does it make you?" Phyllis asked.

"A brother-fucker!" Dawn blurted, burying her face in her hands.

"A what?" Colette shrieked.

"Did you just make that up?" Phyllis asked, smirking.

"That's what I've been reduced to y'all! A fucking brother-fucker!"

Phyllis burst into laughter clapping her hands together. Colette nudged her with her elbow.

"This isn't funny at all, Phyllis." Colette admonished, shaking her head.

Phyllis inhaled and cleared her throat. "I'm sorry for laughing at your pain. It's just that I've never *ever* heard that expression before. But you didn't know that he was your brother."

"*Half*-brother," Colette said again.

"It's disgusting any which way you think about the scenario," Dawn admitted.

"Wasn't it from the beginning?" Colette asked incredulously.

Dawn shot daggers. "I don't need your damn holy-rolling judgment! Do you think I would voluntarily sleep with a family member? Is that what you think of me?"

"No. No. I'm sorry," she reached for her hand, but her gesture was rejected. "That's not what I meant… I meant sleeping with them at the same time."

"Like I said, I don't need your judgment! This whole family can kick rocks and stub a big toe!" Dawn stood up swiftly, snatched her purse from the corner of the sofa and continued, "I know you've been talking about me behind my back. I know you all have your opinions about what I should do with *my* body, but you can shove them up your ass! This is MY life… as screwed up as it is right now, but pretty soon this will all be behind me!"

"Where are you going?" Phyllis asked.

"I swear you all act like you're a bunch of saints!" Dawn continued her rant with tears stinging at the corners of her eyes.

"Dawn, please don't leave," Colette pleaded.

"I'm going to the liquor store for something stronger than wine!"

When she pulled up to the local liquor store, the rain poured from the sky as if it had been locked away, anxious to escape the heavens. The high winds almost made it impossible to see the pavement, but Dawn made a dash for the entrance anyway. Out the corner of her eye, she saw a black Hummer similar to Raffi's, but didn't get a good look as she tried to avoid getting soaked by the heavy rain.

Quit trippin', girl. It's not his truck. Why would he be in this neighborhood anyway?

She made her way over to the vodka aisle and mulled over a variety of flavored brands. Droplets of rain from her jacket began to form small pools of water around her. If she stood there any longer, the employees would need to get a mop. Just as she was about to make a decision on a flavor a familiar voice and scent greeted her.

"You're glowing," he said, drawing closer in her space.

Dawn flinched, inhaling a deep breath. It was only a matter of time that their paths would cross. She even rehearsed in her head exactly how the conversation would carry out, but at that moment, even though her mouth was wide open, not a single word escaped.

"I'm not going to hurt you," Raffi reassured her taking a step back and flashing a friendly smile with beautiful, perfect white teeth. He hoped that would ease some of her concern. "How are you?"

Dawn looked for an escape, but he had her skillfully cornered. If she turned around, she would be back in the storage room with God-knows-who. She shook her head at her luck of leaving a heated discussion with her sisters only to be confronted by the likes of Raffi. "How's your wife?" Dawn countered with a sneer.

The smile on his face was wiped clean immediately and replaced by surprise. "Uhh… well, your best friend has seen better days, actually. She's hanging on… barely. She misses you, too. We all do."

Oh, my God. My friend is actually dying of ovarian cancer. Dawn felt a wave of guilt sweep over her, causing her to tear up unexpectedly. Her hormones had her extra emotional lately and she hated it.

"Are you following me?"

Raffi looked confused. "What? Why would I…"

"Was that you at the hospital?" Dawn demanded. "I thought that I caught a glimpse of you when we were there to see about my mother."

"I'm not following you," Raffi denied. "I just happened to be on that floor at the same time that you were with…"

"Excuse me." Dawn side-stepped him, trying to ease by, but Raffi didn't budge.

"You won't answer my calls or texts. I'm out here in limbo constantly wondering if you're still carrying my child." Raffi placed his hand on her belly and nodded his head.

His ass is following me! Dawn pushed his hand away. “Don’t touch me!”

“Let’s work this out, please.” Raffi begged, clasping his hands together. “We can be a family.”

Still an arrogant bastard! Never did she think he would be bold enough to place a hand on her after their last encounter. The humiliation and shame that came associated with his name was too much for her to bear. She had loved Raffi for a long time when they were teenagers and often fantasized about marrying him, having kids with him, and constantly making love to him. Truth-be-told, if Raffi wasn’t married to her best friend, Chena, she would eventually forgive him and be with him. He had the best sex she had ever experienced, which had become very addictive. The desire, passion and curiosity between them had built up over the years so when they finally had permission to explore… they exploded. Dawn felt a familiar throbbing between her legs as she stared into his eyes.

Fuck this! He tried to kill you! “You’re in limbo? Wow! Let me remind you that the last time you had me cornered like this you almost choked me to death, literally!” Dawn spewed through clenched teeth. “I had to wear sunglasses around my family and everywhere I went for days because my eyes were so red! Now move the hell out of my way, Raffi!”

He looked nervously around to see if anyone had heard what he had done to her. “Dawn, I want to apologize for the way I behaved. I was so foul for putting my hands on a Queen like you. I… I panicked. You drive me crazy. I just didn’t want you to get rid of our baby. That’s *my* seed growing inside of you. I don’t care who you slept with. I know for a fact that’s *my* baby inside of you.” He pointed to her belly with a desperate look on his face. He clasped his hands in front of his face and pleaded. “Please accept my apology. Shiloh misses you terribly. I miss you… every single inch of you. Chena is way more understanding than you think. This was all her idea to begin with, remember? We can work this out as a family, trust me. Please come back to live with us.”

Dawn zipped up her jacket quickly, eased from around him and waved him off. “Don’t worry about that anymore. I just took care of that situation.”

"No you didn't," he refuted, raising a thick eyebrow. "Like I said, you're glowing." A smirk tiptoed across his face as he watched Dawn walk away.

Chapter 19

Blood curdling screams jolted Phyllis from her slumber. She glanced at Damien, who was wrestling with waking up or staying asleep. An elbow jab to his ribs from Phyllis helped him decide to wake up.

"What are you doing?" he growled.

"Did you hear that?" Phyllis snatched the sheet from his warm body and was already on her feet. "Babe! Come with me!"

Phyllis didn't wait for his reply. She placed her feet inside her fuzzy slippers and bolted down the hallway. She burst into the twins' room; they were sound asleep. Then muffled whimpering trailed down the hallway. It was Dawn. Phyllis saw Damien emerge from their bedroom, finally.

"The girls are fine," she whispered, waving him off. "I got it. Go back to bed, babe."

Dawn didn't expect to sleep that night, but thanks to her pregnancy, sleep came quickly and she dreamed. She was in a field of wheat running barefoot in a panic, holding her swollen belly. When she tried to scream for help no sound came out. The long white gown she wore was tattered and muddy as if she had been running for a while, unsuccessfully reaching her destination. She saw a field house ahead and burst through the doors relieved.

Inside was a make-shift hospital with white cots, sheets hanging from the window and three nuns. Fear struck through Dawn as she realized she wasn't safe. It was a setup. They all turned to look at her and told her harmoniously, "We've been expecting you." Then they dragged her to a cot, kicking and screaming and finally strapped her wrists down with canvas belts to the posts of the bed.

The older wrinkled, white nun with dark, piercing eyes said, "Now we must remove that demon seed from your womb." The other two nuns held her knees wide open as the older nun reached inside of her with two bare hands and snatched out her baby. Blood spilled into her gown and the sheets. It was a boy and he wailed as if someone had disturbed his sleep. Another nun frowned at him in disgust and snapped his neck.

"You will never be able to have another child because of your sins." The nuns told her simultaneously.

Dawn finally let out a scream with sound.

After a scream like that, Phyllis didn't bother knocking on the door. She barged into the guest bedroom, flicked on the light to see her sister curled up in a tight ball, whimpering.

"My baby! My baby!" Dawn cried.

"What?" Phyllis asked, walking closer to the bed.

"My baby," Dawn repeated, grabbing her stomach. "They killed my baby!"

Phyllis sat next to her baby sister and rubbed her back gently. "It's okay. It was just a nightmare. Open your eyes and look at me."

Dawn sobbed and shook her head. "It was real. It was so real."

"Look at me, Dawn." Phyllis stroked her hair softly.

Dawn quivered, but finally opened her eyes slowly and turned to look at her sister. "Oh, Phyllis! It was so real! They killed my baby!" She threw her arms around Phyllis and cried.

Phyllis hugged and rocked her, letting her get it all out. Dawn had been plagued with nightmares since they were kids. As the big sister of the three, Phyllis had learned to deal with it over the years. The best way was to console her while she caught her breath. Dawn had always believed that her dreams had deeper meanings. Sometimes, they did come to fruition, like her recurring dream about seeing an old white woman being smothered by a woman with a pillow. In fact, it wasn't a dream at all. When Jonetta finally confessed last Thanksgiving that Dawn's nightmares actually happened when she was a little girl, she was relieved and the nightmares about that stopped.

Now the only way to make this nightmare stop was to take matters into her own hands.

"I cannot have this baby," Dawn confessed her feelings with conviction.

"Listen, I think all of this mess with Mama, her great-aunts, Bishon thought to be dead, his parents getting involved, and you unsure of your next move got your nightmares all tangled up. You don't have to make any rash decisions right now," Phyllis replied softly, holding her sister's hand.

"Yes, I do!" Dawn wiped her tears. "Don't you get it? This baby cannot be born under these circumstances. Regardless of who the father is…neither one of them will ever belong to me. Bishon is far more important to Mama right now than what I'm going through. She is choosing Bishon over me, over all of us!"

"No, she's not…"

"Yes, she is!" Dawn insisted angrily. "She's so thrilled to have a son that couldn't care less about any of us, nor this baby."

"A son that she thought was dead for over forty-years," Phyllis reminded her sister.

Dawn took a moment to reflect on that fact.

"But what if it's not's Bishon's baby?" Phyllis asked softly.

"Raffi isn't a better candidate," Dawn replied, wiping her nose with her sleeve. "That will complicate things with me and Chena… sharing a man, splitting his time between the kids. It won't be fair to anyone."

"I thought they wanted you to move back in with them?"

"Do I look like a Sister-Wife to you?" Dawn snapped. "Oh, my God! My life has become a damn reality show!"

Phyllis tried to reason with her as best as she could. "Listen, there are ways to find out through tests."

Dawn looked at her sister incredulously. "And who has that type of money for genetic testing? That shit is expensive. It's unnecessary anyway."

"Why do you say that?"

"Because I don't ever want to be somebody's mother!"

Later in the afternoon, Phyllis found herself replaying the conversation that she had with her sister. Was being a mother that bad? Or did Dawn have mommy-issues to work through?

After suffering two miscarriages, Lord knows that Phyllis cried, begged and prayed to God to get pregnant. He finally blessed her double for her trouble with twins after four years of trying. Serena and Sabrina were a handful, more than what she had bargained for, but she was grateful to finally be a mother.

She couldn't remember what life was like prior to becoming a mother. What had been deemed important in her life? What were her priorities? Nothing seemed more important than her daughters. What was Dawn doing so important in her life right now? Nothing. *Seemed to be the perfect time to become a mother.* But her sister was hell-bent on terminating her pregnancy. There was no reasoning with Dawn. Her mind was made up.

Phyllis looked at the clock on the wall and knew Damien would be home any minute. She headed to their master bathroom, looked in the mirror and smiled. Her creamy skin glowed, her natural makeup enhanced her beauty, and her hair slicked up in a top knot gave a full view of her strong cheekbones. Phyllis glided her hands down her silhouette and sucked in her stomach. Her waist line was cinched, but she had a FUPA after giving birth to the twins. Even though being thick with curves and tummy pouch was now considered acceptable beauty standards, six years later, it still bothered her. "We gotta work on this. And if exercise doesn't help, then under the knife we go!" She patted her stomach, sprayed perfume on her cleavage, turned off the light and headed downstairs.

Although Damien was rarely in a horny mood when he came home from work, she still liked to look and smell good for him. On a very rare occasion, her fragrance would drive him crazy and he couldn't resist. She was hoping that today would be one of those days. Her sex drive lately was on a high. Unfortunately, Damien couldn't keep up.

When Phyllis rounded the corner of the stairs she could hear Damien mumbling. *There goes our quickie!*

"What's up, babe?"

"I'm tired of working for someone else!" Damien slammed the basement door after he finished placing his work boots on the landing. "I'm ready to do my own thing!"

"Well, hello to you, too." Phyllis planted a kiss on his cheek. She could tell that he was in a bad mood and wanted to get something off of his chest, so she continued to entertain the conversation. "Like what?"

"I don't know," he furrowed his brows and marched towards the kitchen.

Phyllis followed expectantly. "Babe, well you must have an idea. All you need to do is figure out your talent and gift, then everything will fall into place from there."

"Just like that, huh?" Damien replied. "I just get so frustrated with the management that I feel like walking off the job!"

"You just need to keep working until you figure everything out."

Damien snatched the refrigerator door open and reached for a cold beer. "You don't think I know that?" he snarled as he twisted the cap open and took a long swallow. "I wouldn't have all of this pressure on me if you didn't quit your job!"

"Not this again!" Phyllis threw her hands up in the air and began to walk away. Mid-stroll, she decided that this argument was worth the fight and headed back to the kitchen. "You know what? I have a lot on my plate right now with being a housewife, maid, and chauffer. Not to mention my Mama, Dawn and her unborn baby, this new brother of ours and … and … this Facebook opportunity!"

"Yeah, about that Facebook crap, it's gonna be a hard NO for me dawg!" Damien took another swig of his beer.

"Could you drop the Randy Jackson voice? Thanks!" Phyllis rolled her eyes. "This is a great opportunity to have my own cooking show and I'll be getting paid! Why would you be against that?"

"Because I'm not having a camera crew full of men up in my house on a daily basis."

"Is that your only issue about this opportunity for me? Besides, they won't be here on a daily basis, it's once a week and I'll be getting paid!" Phyllis reminded him. "Would you feel better if I had an all-female camera crew? I can request it."

"That's beside the point," Damien waved her off.

"*You* made it a point when you just mentioned it!" Phyllis put her hands on her hips defiantly, while raising her voice out of frustration. If this conversation were to continue there's no telling where her anger might lead her.

"Look, I don't want any strangers up in my house, period. End of story." Damien replied, sensing that his wife was about to explode.

"This conversation is far from over, Damien Washington!" Phyllis watched her husband exit the room and quickly looked for something to throw at the back of his head. *Everything in here just might kill him.*

Chapter 20

In the morning, Jonetta woke up to male voices in hushed tones. She looked around the bedroom and realized she was on the first floor instead of her bedroom upstairs. When she arrived home, the meds kicked in so strong that she didn't even remember entering the first floor bedroom.

Her vision was blurred, but as it became clearer she saw that it was Bishon in the bedroom with her, folding clothes and putting them in the dresser as quietly as he could. Her heart smiled. She watched him for a while before making a sound. She hadn't noticed before, but he was built exactly like his father, Paul King.

Once upon a time, she was in love with his father, but on that day he offered her a ride, it turned so ugly between them. One minute she was flirting, the next minute her face was being smashed into the soil as he took advantage of her. Jonetta often wondered, if he only knew that she had already planned on making love to him eventually, would he still have raped her? In that split second her whole life changed.

The life she had planned was ruined in that frightful moment. Her mother, not believing a word she said, did what she thought was best and sent her away up north to Chicago, far away from her home in Pennsylvania. God only knows what her life would've been like if she hadn't been raped. What type of woman she would have become? What kind of mother could she have been?

One thing was for sure, Jonetta was determined become the best mother, give as much love as she could because God had just given her a second chance. None of her depressing past mattered so much anymore because right now, looking at her son, gave her joy that tears came to her eyes.

"Son," she whispered.

Bishon was startled as she spun around. He immediately dropped the clothing and rushed to her side. "Mama, you're awake."

"Every time I open my eyes, there you are," she replied with a smile in her voice.

Bishon squeezed her hand gently. He smoothed her hair away from her face to get a better look at her. "We have the same nose, the same shape face, and even our smiles match."

Jonetta smiled.

"I see where I get my good teeth from, too," he teased.

Jonetta patted his hand. "Why aren't you at work? I don't want you closing up your dental office on my behalf."

"I have a new office manager. Don't worry about my patients. You're my number one patient right now."

"You never came back to see me again at the hospital. I asked to see you. What happened?"

"Phyllis said that you didn't want any more visitors," Bishon explained.

"That's not true! I asked for you specifically," Jonetta fumed.

"Well, I'm here now," Bishon replied softly and squeezed her hand.

Norman appeared in the doorway with a tray of broccoli cheddar soup and buttery Ritz crackers that he knew Jonetta loved. The aroma filled the room quickly. Jonetta pulled the plush down comforter up and smoothed her hair. She was absolutely sure that she looked God-awful, but still wanted to appear half-way decent instead of looking dead.

"Thought I heard voices in here. I prepared a little something for you to work up your strength," Norman said as he placed the tray on the nightstand next her.

"Is that a rose from my garden?" Jonetta asked as she picked up the pink single rose.

Norman laughed boisterously. "No. I knew you'd have my head if I plucked a rose from your garden."

Jonetta smiled bashfully and replied, "I wouldn't have minded so much…this time."

"I wasn't taking any chances. Know what I mean?"

Norman winked at Bishon.

Bishon nodded and chuckled.

"Oh, don't go scaring my son off," Jonetta chastised Norman. She grabbed Bishon's hand and replied, "I'm not *that* bad. Don't listen to him."

"Nothing and nobody can scare me away from you, Mama." Bishon replied and planted a kiss on her cheek.

"I like the sound of all of that…especially 'Mama'," Jonetta cooed.

"I figured that I should call you what the girls call you," he shrugged.

"You mean your sisters," Jonetta corrected him.

Bishon looked up at Norman to see his reaction. After all, they were his daughters.

Norman nodded with approval. "Whether they like it or not, they are your sisters."

Jonetta furrowed her brows and questioned, "What do you mean by that? I know my daughters are not acting ugly with you. Are they?"

Bishon looked at Norman again for guidance on the conversation.

He shook his head slightly and cleared his throat.

"No, Mama, nothing like that," he lied.

Jonetta exhaled. "Good because the last thing my heart needs is more upsetting news. I just need everyone to open their arms, welcome you into the family and move forward with love and acceptance."

By late afternoon, Jonetta drifted into another deep sleep. Norman took Phyllis up on her offer to help around the house so he could rest as well. Bishon was good company and helpful with Jonetta, but he wasn't about to clean up the house.

"Daughter of mine, you are right on time!" Norman greeted Phyllis with a tight hug. "Let me get these bags. What you got here?"

"Well, I thought since I'm here that I'd make at least two dishes for you and Mama. You know I'm an internet sensation top chef, right?" Phyllis laughed as she arranged the groceries on the counter.

"Yes, I heard all about it and I'm proud of you," Norman planted a kiss on her cheek. "That bookface is gonna make you a star, huh?"

"Facebook," Phyllis laughed. Norman loved teasing them about their social media "addictions", as he called it. "Dad, why don't you go get some rest? Even if you need to take one of Mama's muscle relaxers, nobody would blame you. I know this cannot be easy on you, but your help is here now," Phyllis beamed.

The first floor bathroom door opened and footsteps approached.

"Mama, you should be in bed resting," Phyllis said shaking her head. Her eyes grew wide when she saw it was Bishon approaching the kitchen.

"I'm here to help as well," Bishon announced firmly.

"Dad! What is *he* doing here?" Phyllis fumed.

Norman failed to mention to her that Bishon was also helping out. His intentions were good, but futile.

"He has a name," Bishon remarked and walked closer to Phyllis by the counter. "Phyllis, I'm your brother and I'm not going anywhere. You cannot pretend that this situation doesn't exist because clearly, it does." He spread his arms wide so she could get a good look at him.

"Unfortunately," Phyllis grumbled. "You're our *half*-brother! Why won't you allow us some space to get used to the idea before you go inserting yourself in our lives?"

"You've had your whole life knowing exactly who your mother is! Now, imagine not knowing," Bishon paused for a moment to let his reality sink into Phyllis' mind. "You cannot imagine life any other way, can you? Our mother told me how she specifically asked for me at the hospital. What did you do, Phyllis? You lied saying she didn't want any more visitors. So, now, it's my turn to get to know my mother on my terms, whether you like it or not!" Bishon said fiercely. He had just about enough of Phyllis and her nasty attitude towards him.

"Bishon and Phyllis, lower your voices," Norman interjected sternly. "My God! Your mother is back there trying to get some much needed rest for crying out loud. I know that I can trust the two oldest to behave in an adult manner while I get some rest, too! Right?"

"Of course, Dad," Phyllis conceded. She turned her back as she finished unloading the groceries and exhaled sharply.

Bishon nodded at Norman, "Get some rest. We'll manage."

Once Phyllis knew for sure that her father was in his bedroom she faced Bishon and examined him thoroughly. Maybe a DNA test wasn't necessary after all. He did have features similar to Jonetta's and even his smile was striking like hers. His smooth dark skin glistened as the sun filled the kitchen. She could see the attraction Dawn had; he was very handsome.

"Had I known that you were here, I wouldn't have rushed over here," she admitted. "I didn't see your car in the driveway."

"I parked across the street," Bishon shrugged. "You know how your dad is when it comes to family. He set us up to be here together to help them. I'm here out of love and respect, not to fight with you."

Phyllis nodded and began pulling pans from the pantry along with a chopping board. She had already planned on making tomato, basil and mozzarella stuffed chicken with spring vegetables and a turkey sausage lasagna to last them for the week.

"You need some help? I'm a pretty good cook," Bishon offered.

"In case you hadn't heard, I'm the 'pretty good cook' in this family," Phyllis replied smirking.

"Dawn mentioned it a time or two."

"Listen, about you and my sister, your half-sister," Phyllis eyed him up and down before she chose her next words. "I just need to know what your plans are regarding my family."

Bishon took a seat at the table and buried his face in his hands. He moaned loudly and peeked at Phyllis through his fingers. "You keep saying it's *your* family like you're in sole possession of them. We are all related so this is my family, too. I know it's all screwed up now thanks to me, but, listen, I grew to love Dawn. Now, I just have to love her in a different way."

Phyllis frowned with a disbelieving look on her face. "C'mon now. We both know once you have sexual ties with someone it's hard to break."

Bishon cleared his throat as he let her words sink in. It was true and it was his major regret. "I told Dawn that I don't think it's best to bring a baby into this situation."

"You did what?" Phyllis stopped mid-chop of the zucchini.

"That didn't go over too well," he admitted, squirming in his seat.

"I'm sure it didn't!" Phyllis placed her hand on her hip indignantly. "Here's a Newsflash: Neither a man nor the government has a right to tell a woman what to do with her body. Not now, not ever."

Bishon held up his hands in surrender, "I know. I know. I overstepped my boundaries. I was just thinking about the baby's health."

"I doubt that's all you were thinking about," Phyllis eyed him up and down.

Bishon darted his eyes away from that truth. "Of course, I was thinking about how it would affect all of us, too. This is such a joyous yet disastrous situation for me. I've got my birth mother in my life who loves my presence. Then I've got my mother who raised me who wants more of my presence because she feels threatened. Then I have three sisters who don't want to be in my presence because they feel threatened. I just want to walk away from all of this!" He admitted slouching down in the chair looking dejected.

Phyllis could tell that any given moment he was about to break and she was not emotionally equipped to give a damn right now.

"Here," she said holding out a chopping knife. "You can help me cut up these vegetables. It usually relieves stress for me."

Bishon smiled and gladly walked over to the counter to assist with making dinner. “Phyllis to the rescue.”

Chapter 21

Colette watched Owen carefully as he played with their children at the park. Squeals filled the warm air as he chased them around the park pretending to be a monster. He was a good father for the most part. He was also a terrible provider, a terrible husband and a terrible person to her. Unfortunately, she couldn't separate any of it. All the bad he had done during their relationship outweighed any good deeds.

How could she not know that they were never officially married? How could he pretend to be her husband all these years? What type of person would do this to someone? Suddenly, fear struck through her spine as she realized that she didn't really know Owen at all. *Anybody watching would think he's father of the year!* She sat seething on the park bench, pushing the stroller back and forth to soothe Delilah. She had just finished nursing and burping her when she saw Owen walking in her direction.

Colette inhaled sharply and rolled her eyes when he got too close for her comfort. "What do you want?"

"Why you sitting over here like somebody stole your bike?" he teased. "You don't have to be here watching us like I'm gonna kidnap them or something. But since you are here stalking me, we gotta talk."

"What is there to talk about?" Colette asked, dismissing all of his petty insinuations.

"Well, first of all, I wanted to tell you how sexy you looked over here breastfeeding my daughter. I'm kinda tempted to get some of that for myself. Yours tastes way better than Shante's for damn sure!" He rubbed his hands together and a sly grin spread across his face.

"Those days are over. We are done, remember? We never were married. All of your rights and privileges are revoked!"

"I still have rights to see my kids!" Owen shouted. With such a quick temper, it didn't take long for his true colors to show.

Colette looked around, embarrassed by his outburst. "Take me to court and we'll deal with it there, along with child support."

"Court?"

"Yeah, you know the place where the judge sits on a bench and makes a determination on the case before him," she replied sarcastically. "I'm so sure with your track record of domestic violence that you know the place."

"You're such a BITCH!"

"Tell it to the judge," Colette said nonchalantly. She directed her attention to their children who were running around the playground with some other children that they knew from school. Colette waved to them and smiled.

"I heard Dawn is pregnant by y'all brother or some shit like that. Yeah, that's right. Cornell told me all about your nasty family drama. I'm sure the judge won't think that your family is the best for *my* kids. Sounds like a real unhealthy environment to me," Owen replied, smirking. "Maybe I'll tell *that* to the judge!" He finally had the upper hand and he liked it.

Colette squinted her eyes, mustered the meanest expression on her face, stood almost nose to nose with Owen, pointing her finger in his face and snarled, "If you ever think about taking my kids from me it'll be the worst decision you have ever made! You will regret the moment your Mama moved to my neighborhood when we were kids. I can guarantee on everything I love you will be sorry!"

"Ohhhh weee! Look at you! Getting all big and bad with me!" Owen applauded and laughed. "Is that a threat? Are you threatening me, Colette? It's actually turning me on!" He grabbed his crotch and squeezed her right breast at the same time.

"Move out of my way, Owen!" Colette shoved his shoulder. She maneuvered the stroller past him and called for her children to get in the car.

They moaned and complained about leaving the park so suddenly. "We just got here," Cornell whined.

"Can we say good-bye to Daddy?" Lydia asked.

Colette reluctantly nodded and replied, "Hurry up." She watched as the three of them dashed towards Owen, smothering him in hugs that he didn't deserve. *Bastard.*

Later that evening, Colette decided to phone Dawn. It had been really bothering her that Owen knew about their family situation. Cornell admitted that he called his dad from the hospital when all the commotion was happening. How could she be mad at her son? It wasn't his fault that they were feuding in front of the kids. But now that Owen knew, she didn't put it past him to use it against her in court. He had reached a new low with that threat.

"Hey sis," Dawn answered. She sounded as if she was already dozing off.

"That baby got you sleepy, huh?"

"Is that what it is? I'm tired all the time," she said yawning loudly. "I feel like I've been hit by a truck and drugged!"

"Pregnancy-sleep is some of the best sleep that I've ever had in my life," Colette admitted and laughed.

"Ohhhh! So, is that why you keep having these kids?" Dawn teased.

Colette chuckled. "If I had known that I'd be a single parent, I would've never had a single child."

"Really?"

"Oh, I'm sorry, girl." Colette regretted sharing her truth when she realized it came out heartless.

"For what? I appreciate the honesty," Dawn replied unbothered. "I don't plan on being a single parent, ever."

"Wait. What are you saying? You aren't going to marry our half-brother, are you?"

Dawn laughed incredulously. "No! I'm saying that I'm not going to be a mother, ever."

There was an awkward moment of silence. Colette tightened the sash on her robe and swallowed hard.

"Dawn…"

"It's my body…"

"Of course! But that's not where I was going with the conversation," Colette explained. "Listen, Owen knows about all of this and he threatened to take me to court over it to get custody of the kids."

"What!"

"Yes. He's an asshole!"

"He's a manipulative motherfucker!" Dawn shouted.

Colette held the phone away from her ear for a second. "Yes. He stooped really low, but I think he'll bring it up in court for sure just to spite me. What if the judge agrees with Owen about an unfit family environment? I cannot lose my kids to him! I don't know what I would do without my kids," Colette lamented. "They are my whole world. All of this drama is just breaking my heart."

"Colette, calm down. You're letting this asshole work you up over nothing! My situation holds no bearing on the safety and well-being of *your* kids," Dawn reassured her. "Besides, by the time you go to court, I won't be pregnant anymore."

"I'm sorry to hear that, sis."

"My mind is made up," Dawn sighed. "Now get some rest. I'm about to doze off."

Colette ended the call and put it on vibrate. It was getting late, but she still had to clean the kitchen and get the kids settled for bed.

"Cornell!" she called upstairs. "Start the bath water and get the pajamas out of the drawer."

"Okay, Mama," he answered.

Colette waited for a moment until she heard the water running in the tub. Satisfied, she checked on Delilah who was sleeping in the playpen. *She's so precious.* Some music would help her clean faster, so she turned on Pandora while she put away the cups and plates. Her finger ran across a chip on a plate to the set Aunt Georgia adored. She sucked her teeth. *I should've never let the kids use these plates.* Before she could decide if she should fuss at the kids, the doorbell rang.

Peering out the window, she became angry and snatched open the door. "What are you doing here?" she growled.

"I came to apologize," Owen said, humbly.

"At nine o'clock at night?"

"Daddy!" Lydia yelled from the top of the stairs and came running down. Ruthie and Cornell followed right behind her.

"Shhhhh! Before you wake up the baby!" Colette fussed. "Look at all this ruckus you're causing, Owen."

Owen ignored her, stepped inside, opened his arms and hugged them warmly as if he just hadn't seen them earlier.

"What are y'all doing up?"

"We're getting in the tub now," Cornell said.

Owen stood up and eyed Colette who had a dish towel in her hand, hair disheveled and tired eyes. He figured she was behind on their regular schedule so he offered to help out. "Come on. Let's get these baths and get in the bed. Don't y'all have school tomorrow?"

"Yes! But I don't want a bath," Ruthie whined.

"Obey your father," Colette said, pointing upstairs. "All of you. Go upstairs and get ready for bed with your Daddy."

Colette watched them all climb the stairs and couldn't believe it herself, but she was grateful for his last-minute help. It was one less thing she had to do tonight. By the time the children were bathed and tucked into bed, Colette was done with the kitchen and Owen had reemerged.

"Thanks. It's late now. I'm sure you should be heading home." Colette leaned against the sink and folded her arms.

"No problem. I'm their Daddy and always will be," he said, pulling out a chair at the kitchen table.

"Well, I should get to bed, too." Colette hinted.

"Look, like I said earlier, I came here to apologize. Well, Shante told me I should apologize to you because you know I ain't good at apologizing and shit," he admitted, leaning back in the chair.

"Oh, did she tell you do it right now? This late at night?" Colette rolled her eyes. "Does she even know that you're here?"

"I'm a grown ass man," Owen laughed. "Listen, I see you're overwhelmed without me here. So, why don't I come by three times a week to help you out?"

Colette frowned. "I don't think so, Owen. Where do you even come up with these ideas? I know Shante won't approve of that!"

"Hey, if it were up to me, we'd all be living under one roof!"

"Do I look like a sister-wife to you?" Colette scoffed.

"No. But you look like you could use my help," Owen said, reaching for her hand. "Let me help you. It's either that or I gotta take Cornell to live with me and my other son. You can raise our daughters."

"What?! Stop threatening to take any of my children from me!" she said fiercely, snatching her hand back. "Have you lost your mind?"

"Then let me help you out a few days out the week. I've thought about this. I don't want my kids growing up without their Daddy in the house. It fucks kids up later on in life. Trust me. You don't want our kids out here fucked up, do you?"

Colette thought about it for a second. *Why should I do this all by myself? A few days a week won't hurt.* "You know what, let's give it a try. But you will not be spending the night. We have to set boundaries. You'll only be here to help me out with the kids."

"Of course. I don't need to spend the night to spend time with my own kids and help you out," Owen replied, tugging at the hem of her sleeve. "What is this? Silk or something?"

Colette smiled sheepishly. "Yes, it is." Aunt Georgia had so many beautiful clothing, including lingerie, robes, and slippers. Colette thought it was a shame to let it all go to waste, so she chose a few items for herself. The black robe with huge, red dahlia flowers on it was her favorite robe. Besides, she had never felt silk on her skin before and she loved it.

"Looks and feels good on you," he said, sliding his hand down her arm. "I miss you, girl."

Colette looked away before he could manipulate her. Owen stood up and guided her chin back in his direction.

"Stop." Colette moved his hand from her face.

"I don't wanna fight no more." Owen leaned in closer and kissed her on the forehead. "You know you my number one girl. None of that other shit is ever gonna change that. You hear me?"

Colette began to throb between her legs. She knew everything he was saying was bullshit, but it sounded good and felt good. His touch had always made her weak. It had been months since she had been touched. Owen was the only man she knew. His fresh scent indicated that he had showered before he arrived at the house. It was intoxicating as she inhaled. She leaned back on the counter, closed her eyes and exhaled.

Owen had seized that split second to untie her robe and open it, exposing her full breasts. He gently grabbed her by the neck, pulled her closer by the waist, and fondled her breasts. Before she could refuse his touch, he dove in like a hawk capturing its prey. The strong pull from his mouth and squeezing motion had her aroused. She wanted him to stop because she knew it was over between them, but her longing to be touched won the battle.

"Owen," Colette moaned, grabbing his hair.

"Gimme my milk, girl. You taste so damn good." He moaned with pleasure as he released one nipple and devoured the other. Squeezing and sucking like it was his last meal, Colette panted with pleasure. Eventually, his hand found its way between her legs and then his tongue soon followed.

"Fuck me!"

"That's exactly what I came here to do."

Chapter 22

"You are still a mother!"
"If you do this, you'll just be a mother of a dead baby!"

"Choose life!"

"Pro-Life!" The crowd began to chant as Dawn passed by anxiously.

"I don't have a choice!" Dawn yelled to the crowd.

"You have a choice not to kill your unborn child!" A protestor shouted in her ear.

"Don't kill your baby!" another pleaded and pulled her by the arm.

"God will make you pay unless you repent of your sins!" A priest shouted towards her direction.

"Fuck off!" Dawn spewed at the priest and snatched away from the protestor. He gasped, jerked his neck and gestured the sign of the cross with his fingers.

"Dawn! Don't engage with these protestors! For heaven's sake!"

The protestors and religious fanatics continued to shout, reciting Bible scriptures as a persuasion tactic. Their faces were so twisted and full of hate instead of compassion. Dawn was convinced that they were sent on the behalf of Satan rather than the Christ they claimed died for all sins.

"Why did you bring me to this clinic?" Dawn hissed.

"This is where Mama brought me." Phyllis shrugged. "It's always chaotic like this at this facility. Just ignore them."

"Well, thanks a lot for the warning!" Dawn glared at her sister. "Dammit! I just want to go home!"

"But you said…"

"I know what I said, Phyllis!" Dawn walked towards the entrance quickly with her head down, dark shades on with hair covering her face as much as it could.

Phyllis matched her pace, shook her head and grabbed her sister's elbow. "Next time you make a deal with the devil, make sure you get it in writing, girl!"

"They'd be better off throwing lemons and tomatoes!" Dawn remarked as she gave the angry crowd a last glance before entering the building.

After Dawn checked in, she took a seat besides Phyllis in the waiting area. She surveyed the room quickly to make sure she didn't see anyone that might know her. She exhaled a sigh of relief once she was satisfied with all the unfamiliar faces. *Hell, we're all here for the same reason anyway! None of these heffas can judge me!*

"I hope this doesn't take too long. I have to take the girls to gymnastics today."

"Oh, I'm sorry if I'm causing a delay in your schedule today," Dawn snarled. "You're free to go. I can always call an Uber."

"Trust me, after this is all over, the last person you want to be around is a complete stranger." Phyllis sighed as she looked at Dawn's expression on her face. She was scared. "I didn't mean it like that, sis. I'm not going anywhere. I'm just thinking out loud about everything that I need to do today after the girls get home from school and Damien gets home from work. He's all upset because Owen sent him a link to my Facebook video where I popped the girls on the hand. Now he thinks DCFS will get involved if anyone reports me. So of course, he wants me to stop filming my cooking show. All because Owen is a miserable son of a bitch and a Facebook snitch! I swear, my nerves are bad! And folks expect me to stay sober? Yeah, right!"

"Owen is doing the most right now!" Dawn replied.

"What else has he done?"

"He's threatening to use my situation against Colette in court so he can get custody of the kids."

"Has he lost his mind completely?" Phyllis fumed. "I swear that man isn't happy unless he's making other people miserable."

"Now he won't have anything to hold over head," Dawn said matter-of-factly.

"Is that why you were in a rush to get here?"

Dawn shook her head. "Nah. I had already made it up in my mind to get this done sooner than later. Now everyone's problems will be solved once this is over."

Phyllis squeezed her hand. "I'm sorry you feel that way. I'm sorry you're in this situation. I hope you're making this decision for you and not the family."

"Trust me, I'm doing this for me." Dawn began to check her iPhone for messages. She hadn't been as responsive to text messages and phone calls lately unless it was from her sisters or parents. A message from her father caught her attention.

Norman: You are on my mind daughter. I remember the day you were born. We couldn't agree on a name. It was cold and raining. It had been raining for a whole week. But, the weather man said the next day at dawn, the sun would be shining. Dawn of a new day. That's when we knew that would be your name. I LOVE YOU!

Dawn smiled at his thoughtful text. She sent back a heart emoji. Even though it bothered her that he was in contact with Bishon for her mother's sake, she knew that it was jealousy on her part. Dawn had been jealous that her father's concern was for her mother's first-born child instead of their last-born child who needed the most attention right now.

It felt like she was in competition with her lover and she was not happy about it all. She had planned to follow her mother's advice about telling Bishon that the baby was his to secure her financial future until they all found out that he was their brother.

The family was fractured. They all wanted to smooth things over, embrace their brother, but the fact that he had been sleeping with Dawn made it awkward for everyone. After Labor Day, Dawn was going to make some moves.

"Anyway, Dawn, you aren't *that* far along. Your procedure shouldn't take that long or it might judging by the number of women here now. That's all I'm saying." Phyllis announced breaking her train of thought.

"I'm aware of that, thanks." Dawn glanced around the waiting room and spotted one women whose belly was protruding. *She must be like six months pregnant. My God!*

"Well, what did Raffi or Bishon have to say about your decision?" Phyllis had been dying to know how they reacted when she told them that she was coming to the clinic today.

"I haven't spoken to Raffi since … It's been a while," Dawn rolled her eyes in disgust. "I talked to Chena, though. I led her to believe that I was keeping the baby so Raffi would back off. She wasn't happy about that news, though. Honestly, at this point I don't give a shit!"

"I guess she wouldn't be too happy about her husband cheating and having another child on the way! Who would?"

Dawn jerked her neck and frowned at her sister's opinionated rhetoric. "Let's be clear on this. Raffi was not cheating on Chena. It was her idea that we hook up in the first place. We were just fulfilling her dying wishes. Keep up, Phyllis."

"A modern day Geisha, huh? All of y'all belong on somebody's reality show!" Phyllis scoffed.

Dawn rolled her eyes and grunted. "When I went to audition for a reality show everybody was against it. Especially you, Phyllis! Remember?"

"What about Bishon?" Phyllis asked instead of acknowledging Dawn's accurate recollection.

"What about him?" Dawn retorted.

"He has a right to know, too."

Dawn stared at her sister in disbelief. *She is the blackest-blonde that I know! I should've just come alone. I don't need this shit from her!*

"Oh, yeah? Well, I had a right to know that he was my fucking brother!" Dawn retorted. Her last comment drew attention from women sitting close by.

"Would you lower your damn voice?"

"Would you stop interrogating me?"

A side door opened and a woman in a white lab coat appeared holding a clipboard. "Dawn Miller," she said her name loudly.

Dawn gathered her purse and stood, "Yeah. That's me."

"We need to get your vitals," she announced, pushing the door open wider with her hip. "Follow me."

Dawn snatched her purse and whisked past her sister.

Back in room 11, she stared at the ceiling, trying to steady her labored breathing as she lied flat on her back on the gurney in the cold, sterile room. Her gown was white, the doctor's stool was white, and even all the walls were painted white. *These walls should be red, like blood, like the fiery entrance to hell because that's where we're all going!* She slapped her hand on her forehead and whimpered.

"It'll be fine," the nurse said, patting her arm. "I'm going to take your blood pressure, start your I.V. and give you something so you can drift off to sleep after the doctor is done with your consultation."

Dawn had a look of confusion on her face. "Wait… I … ummm…I thought you were only going to take my vitals. I wanted to give my sister a few of my items before… Wait just a minute. You're about to start the procedure now?" Dawn ran her fingers through her mangled hair nervously.

She wanted to talk to Phyllis more before the procedure. She had a whole list of final wishes written down just in case she never woke up again from this procedure. A girl she grew up with, Nadine Mansour, had an abortion at 16-years-old and died right there on the operating table. Her mother never even knew that she was pregnant in the first place. Dawn always wondered what their last conversation had been, or where Nadine had told her mother that she was going that day. Surely, her mother believed whatever lie Nadine had told her only to receive a call from the hospital that her only daughter died.

"When you wake up, it'll all be over and you can go home." The nurse replied like a robot, ignoring Dawn's confusion. Her voice was whiny, plastered and hollow as if she were reading from a script.

That only irritated Dawn. "Is that what you tell all the women who come here to make a life or death choice?" Dawn snapped at the nurse.

The nurse met Dawn's piercing eyes and flashed a smile as she tied a blue rubber tourniquet around her arm. "You'll be fine. Now make a fist." She instructed Dawn as she poked her with a needle.

Dawn winced and sucked her teeth. *This bitch did that on purpose!* The nurse taped the needle down to her skin firmly and told Dawn that the doctor would be with her shortly.

After the nurse left, Dawn heard Aunt Georgia's voice loud and clear. "Babies are a blessing from God." A chill raced down her spine, the hairs on her arms raised at full attention. She sat straight up. *I can't do this!* Dawn swung her legs around the gurney, looking frantically around the sterile room for her purse. Before she could lunge for it and make her exit, the doctor entered the room. *Shit!*

On the car ride home, Dawn was quiet mainly because of the drugs. Thoughts of guilt raced through her mind, but what else was she supposed to do? *I did the right thing.*

"Of course you did," Phyllis said.

"Huh?"

"You said you did the right thing and I'm agreeing with you," Phyllis explained.

"I said that out loud?" Dawn shook her head. "I'm trippin' out over here."

"Now you don't have to worry about any drama with our new-found brother or Raffi with his crazy ass! And you know Chena was only going to be jealous once that baby arrived and miraculously be free of cancer," Phyllis babbled on as if she had given it much thought. "The last thing you want is a mentally retarded baby, Dawn. You know that's exactly what would happen if it was Bishon's baby. The bloodline was just too close. You got rid of your drama by getting rid of that baby. You did the right thing, sis. Definitely."

"Do you ever listen to yourself?"

"What? What did I say wrong now?"

Dawn shook her head in disbelief. She reached in her purse for the prescriptions the doctor wrote for pain and infection. "Here," she handed it to Phyllis as she pulled up to the pharmacy window.

"Did he give you the good stuff?"

Oh, my God! Get me outta this car! "Phyllis, please… I need silence."

***

"The girls are finally out for the count," Phyllis announced as she dramatically dragged herself into the living room like a zombie. "What are you watching?"

"A movie."

Phyllis put her hands on her hips. "I can see that, smart ass!" She plopped down on the sofa next to Dawn, placing her phone on the coffee table.

"I'm just doing a Netflix and chill, but if you're going to interrupt." Dawn picked up the remote control and turned the television to a local channel. "I'll catch up on that later."

Phyllis chuckled at that bratty move. "I was actually just going to join you in silence. You know? Sister-time with some wine."

"Well, where's the wine?" Dawn teased.

"You're such a brat. I'll be right back." Phyllis tossed the pillow towards Dawn's face, but she blocked it.

"You're such a typical big sister." Dawn stuck out her tongue and turned her attention back to the television.

"Stay tuned for an all new episode of The Real Mistresses of Atlanta. You don't want to miss!" The television announced.

Dawn repositioned herself and cleared her throat. The intro music played, flashing faces of the cast, and lo and behold, Gideon made it on the show. *Good for you Gideon!*

"Damn! I could've totally played up this pregnancy on this show. People would've been speculating who I'm pregnant by and everything!" she sucked her teeth.

"What was that?" Phyllis asked from the kitchen.

"Nothing," Dawn mumbled. "Nothing at all."

"On second thought, I don't think you're supposed to be drinking alcohol while taking antibiotics," Phyllis teased, emerging from the kitchen.

"Girl, if you don't bring that wine over here."

"Okay, but don't blame me if you have a setback."

Phyllis handed her sister a glass of Merlot, clinked glasses together and took a sip.

"My whole life has been a setback since I left New York, refused to marry Vine, and moved back to this Godforsaken city."

Phyllis jerked her neck and placed her glass on the coffee table. "Wait a minute. I just so happen to love this 'Godforsaken city'. Chicago raised us! Don't ever forget that."

Dawn laughed and nodded. "True."

"But, rewind a minute. Do you actually regret not marrying Vine and moving to Atlanta?"

Dawn took a long swallow from her glass emptying it and placed it next to Phyllis' glass. She was going to need all the courage she could muster for this conversation. The wine raced through her body like it was in a hurry to get her drunk. Before she could answer the reality show began. Dawn picked up the remote and turned up the volume.

"Look, there's my friend, Gideon. We were in the modeling industry together. He slayed makeup and hair. Had us all looking beat to the Gawds! I ran into him at the auditions in Atlanta," Dawn turned the volume up. "He made it on the show. I walked out because of my encounter with Vine had my nerves wrecked, and the lack of support from my family didn't help. So, in that moment I thought that I was above being on a show like this after all."

"You are!" Phyllis argued. "You're a Top Model! Not some side chick trick looking to be famous on a trashy reality show!"

"Look at me now though. I'm sitting here on your sofa doing nothing with my life! I'm literally recovering from an abortion for Christ's sake!" Dawn threw her hands in the air. "What if I had just went through with the auditions? What if I just would've accepted Vine's marriage proposal? None of this would've ever happened."

Phyllis squeezed her hand and replied, "Better is coming for you. It's only *up* from here, sis."

"You better believe it!"

Chapter 23

The courtroom was jam packed with men and women who were waiting their turn to be heard by the judge regarding child support or the lack thereof. Even though everyone in her family kept reassuring her that Owen didn't stand a chance of gaining custody of their four children, Colette was nervous. Owen could bring up anything in her past to discredit her as a fit mother in front of the judge.

He was the type of man that would avoid paying child support at all costs. On numerous occasions he told her that any man paying child support through the courts was a punk. "Real men handle theirs outside of the courtroom! Real men don't allow the government to tell them how to provide for their own family!

Real men lay down the law!" He had said during a drunken rant about his desire to have numerous children and supporting them for a lifetime. He wanted a legacy. Of what? Colette wasn't quite certain since he was always careless with his money.

At the time, Owen only had one son and he wanted more children, especially sons, but Colette was done having children. The answer to her refusal to have more kids was to have more children with another woman. His plan worked and he had another son.

Shante will be sitting right here in a few years when he's done using her. Colette shook her head at the thought of Owen having another child. She was disgusted by their whole situation.

Now they were standing before a judge for the exact reason that qualified him as a man, in his eyes. Colette feared that he would fight dirty just to prove his point about paying child support. But she secretly hoped the recent night they shared would make him behave. She had agreed to the three days a week and she had allowed him to please her body. And she'd do it all again to keep her children and keep the peace. *God, please let him only discuss visitation today.*

"I didn't know they had a separate courtroom for unwed parents for child support," Norman whispered to Colette.

Colette shrugged, "Me either, Dad. But then again, I didn't know that I wasn't married."

Norman grunted and leaned back on the hard wooden bench. He scanned the small, stuffy courtroom for Owen, but didn't see his unmistakable face. "You just might be in luck today if he doesn't show up." Norman had a hint of happy in his voice.

Colette scanned the room and inhaled sharply once she saw Owen enter the courtroom. He looked so polished in a button down shirt that was actually tucked in his slacks. His long, curly black hair was slicked back into a neat ponytail at the nape of his neck. His face was free from any stubble that she had just seen a few weeks ago. Owen was clean shaven and dapper. His new woman, Shante was right beside him wearing a navy blue three-piece suit, with soft yellow blouse, nude stilettos and a black Tory Burch handbag.

Colette, feeling even more insecure, looked down at her appearance and frowned. She didn't make any effort to appear presentable. *What was I thinking?* Her morning consisted of getting the children fed and out the door for school, dropping Delilah off with Dawn, rushing to get back home to gather documents and mentally preparing for her case to be heard. She didn't bother to change out of her Reeboks, yoga pants and overstretched t-shirt that had spit-up stains on the shoulder. The only thing she was focused on was getting child support for their four children.

"Don't worry sweetheart," Norman patted her knee. "Once he opens his mouth, the judge will see straight through him."

Colette exhaled and rolled her eyes. She looked at her paperwork and silently recited her plea. In a manila envelope she had a stack of receipts from groceries, utility and medical bills from the past year when he decided to quit his job. With sweaty palms, she grabbed her father's hand and squeezed it. Norman squeezed back and straightened his back confidently.

The bailiff stood in front of the courtroom, calling for everyone's attention. "Okay, folks, listen up. We have a packed house today. If you do not have a case to be heard, please exit and wait in the hallway."

Nobody budged.

The bailiff waited for a moment and tried again, "If you are here for moral support, wait in the hallway!"

Grumbling and shuffling of the feet began to fill the once quiet room. Colette and Norman exchanged glances.

"Dad, don't leave me here alone."

"Sweetheart, I don't have a choice. Let's not make matters worse by disobeying the court."

Colette gulped hard and broke into a sweat.

"Dad…"

"I'll be right in the hallway waiting for you, I promise. Stay strong." Norman stood and walked stiffly towards the exit. He stopped in his tracks once he got to Owen and stared him down for at least 10 seconds before he left the courtroom.

Colette made sure that she saw Shante leave the courtroom. If her father had to leave then she needed to leave as well.

As soon as the courtroom cleared the bailiff announced, "All rise! The honorable Judge Leonard Jamison is proceeding."

The judge entered the courtroom and took his seat. To

Colette's surprise, he was a middle aged, black man who favored one of Owen's uncles. He was handsome with salt and pepper wavy hair and creamy skin, but she wasn't getting good vibes from him the moment he took a seat.

"Court is now in session," the bailiff declared.

Colette must've sat another 40 minutes before the judge called her case. By that time, nerves, an empty stomach and a slight headache had made a permanent impact.

She walked woodenly towards the judge's bench and stood behind her court appointed attorney. Owen was doing the same but with confidence. His eyes burned straight through Colette and she felt it. The meek smile she gave him sent a clear message: *Please play nice today.* But he didn't return the smile.

Instead of listening intently, her thoughts wandered as the judge and the court appointed attorney exchanged words. Colette thought about the good times they shared over the years. Everywhere they went, Owen seemed proud that she was his wife, but now that she thought about it, he never introduced her as his wife. Colette inhaled sharply as she let that sink in.

"Mrs. Aldridge," her attorney called her name. "How would you like to proceed?"

Colette cleared her throat, "My name is Colette Miller. Owen Aldridge, the father of my children, recently informed me that we were never married. So if it pleases the court, please address me as Colette Miller."

The judge sat back in his chair astounded by the news Colette just shared. "Be that as it may, *Ms. Miller*, that is another day, another courtroom, another judge who will sort that out for you. Right now we need to know if you will agree to the terms of joint custody with your husband… excuse me, the father of your children."

"No, I don't agree to joint custody," Colette replied fiercely.

All eyes were fixated on her.

"State your case, Ms. Miller," the judge said and sat back with a smirk on his face.

"This is not a game. My children are not pawn. They are not for sale either," Colette began.

"What are you talking about?" Owen asked.

The judge slammed his gavel. "Mister Aldridge, another outburst and I will put you out of this courtroom. Attorney Graves, please advise your client."

His attorney whispered in his ear for a few seconds, Owen nodded and exhaled.

"Your Honor, we agreed to visitation three times a week at my house. I am the mother of our four children. I have been providing for them ever since Owen decided to quit his job at the city, leave us for another woman and then he had another baby with her. I have receipts of all the bills and groceries," Colette began to open the envelope, but the judge put a halt to that.

"That won't be necessary, Ms. Miller. I believe you," the judge said. "How have you been providing for the children?"

"Through government and family assistance," Colette answered.

"Do you currently work, Ms. Miller?"

"No," Colette replied and hung her head.

"Are you in school, Ms. Miller?"

"No."

Owen leaned towards his attorney, whispered and nodded.

"Your Honor," Owen's attorney spoke. "My client is currently employed with the City of Chicago. He lives in a home suitable enough to accommodate all of his children. In addition, he is able to sufficiently provide with a two-income household. Therefore, my client would like full custody."

"Full custody!?" Colette exclaimed. "Absolutely not!" The judge slammed his gavel several times. "There will be no more outbursts from either of you! I will throw you out!" he threatened for the final time.

"Calm down," Colette's state appointed attorney whispered firmly. "Let me do my job."

Colette fought back tears and began kegel exercises because she felt like her bladder was about to betray her at any second. She looked at Owen with absolute confusion. *What are you doing? We had an agreement!*

"Mr. Aldridge, you would need substantial evidence to prove that Ms. Miller is an unfit and unstable parent. Are you prepared to do that today?"

"Yeah! Ummm…I mean…I am, your honor," Owen

replied confidently. "My attorney has all the documents to prove that Ms. Colette Miller is mentally unstable and unfit to raise our four children." He nodded towards his attorney who proceeded to pull documents from a red folder in front of him.

"Your honor, I have dates and receipts for medication that Ms. Miller has used and maybe still using. We also have reason to believe that Ms. Miller intentionally aborted her last child with my client by throwing herself down a flight of stairs. Furthermore, I have a written statement from my client claiming that Ms. Miller tried to commit suicide three years ago. Lastly, my client is also seeking child support upon granting him full custody. For these reasons, your honor, we are filing for full custody."

Chapter 24

Over the last few weeks, Bishon had been checking on Jonetta twice a week. He would've visited more if it weren't for his dental office hours. Working kept his mind from wandering too far off in the deep end. His mother and father had invited him to dinner at their house on several occasions, but he declined each time. The free time that he had belonged to Jonetta. They had so much catching up to do.

Lately, he had trouble sleeping thanks to all the questions he had yet to ask. When Dawn sent him a text in the middle of the night saying: "It's done" he almost vomited. He had no idea that she had scheduled an appointment for an abortion. He would've been there for her. He would've taken her. Why didn't she tell him?

A tingle shot through his spine as he recalled Dawn telling him that he wasn't the only one she was sleeping with at the time. Bishon didn't respond to the text. Instead, he toiled with the thought of her with another man. Was she passionate with him, too? Did she pour her soul into their sex like she did with him? Or did she truly have all of that saved up for him? It didn't matter. He tried to shoo the thoughts away as quickly as they came. Dawn was his half-sister. He had to train his mind not to care about her in that way anymore, but he was failing miserably.

The fact of the matter was, the biggest problem weighing on his spirit was now over. He should've felt like he could breathe a little easier knowing that Dawn wasn't going to give birth to his child. But he didn't. He should've been relieved that he didn't have to wait in anguish for another eight months to find out if he was the father of her child. But he wasn't. Instead he felt like he was the root cause of her final decision. He felt guilty for having unprotected sex. He felt responsible for the pain she was going through post-procedure. It made him sick to know that he was the reason a child's life ended before it even began.

Bishon gripped the steering wheel tight while sitting at a red light. His grip became slippery as his palms became sweaty. As his thoughts raced, beads of sweat began to appear across his forehead. He was literally making himself sick. "I should've kept my mouth shut!" He hit the steering wheel repeatedly until a blaring horn broke him from his rage. The light had turned green.

Once Bishon arrived to visit Jonetta, he had already made up in his mind that today would be the day he got answers. Everything he knew about himself gave him doubts now. Who was he, really? Where did he get his traits and personality from? Was it really a reflection of Stanton and Barbara, or did he act more like his biological father? What other characteristics did he have from him other than his physical features? Did Jonetta have any pictures of him that she could share?

All of those thoughts had been racing around in his head for weeks and only Jonetta could provide any insight. It was eating at him so much that he almost pulled the wrong tooth from a patient. He needed a vacation, but not before he received some answers. Bishon took a seat on the sofa near Jonetta and study her for a moment. Usually, after her physical therapy sessions, she was extremely tired, but thankfully, her appointment was two days ago. From what he could tell, she was in a good mood and feeling up for conversation.

Jonetta turned down the volume to the television when Bishon finally took a seat. She was always happy to see his face. Even though he favored his biological father, he had his own unique features. Bishon had kind eyes and a welcoming smile.

Those traits made it easy to talk to him. But lately, he hadn't flashed those pearly whites and Jonetta noticed.

"Something is bothering you, isn't it? You can talk to me about whatever is bothering you, son," Jonetta said, reaching for his hand.

Bishon squeezed her hand and let go as he collected his thoughts. He began, "You have no idea the regret I feel about everything," Bishon admitted. "Sometimes, I wish that I would've kept my mouth closed."

"I know this is heavy for you and all of us," Jonetta said softly, patting his knee. "But I am so glad you did your research and found me. It may not be the ideal result you wanted, but still…we have each other now."

"The result that I was expecting was to find out my biological mother was dead by now," Bishon admitted. "So this is much better than what I imagined… except…"

"Except the part about Dawn being your half-sister?"

"And that you suffered a stroke from my news."

Jonetta chuckled and waved him off. "Oh, please. I was bound to have a stroke the way all of the other drama was unfolding."

"Dawn had the abortion," Bishon said and bowed his head.

"She told me. Quite frankly, I'm so glad she did," Jonetta confessed.

Bishon jerked his head up and stared at her in silence for a moment. *What kind of mother would say something like that?* "Why would you say that? It was your grandchild that you'll never get to meet and quite possibly my child!"

"I said it because Dawn was out here being a floozy!" Jonetta replied without batting an eyelash. "There was no sense in bringing a child in that disastrous situation. You should be glad it's over now."

"Well, if you're going to judge her, then you might as well judge me, too." Bishon was becoming defensive and frustrated.

Jonetta shook her head. "No. You're not to blame, son. I'm sure Dawn seduced you."

"No, she didn't!" Bishon countered. He felt his face flush, he was becoming angry hearing Jonetta talk about Dawn that way. *What type of mother talks this way about her own child?* He felt a strong urge to defend her, "The day she came to my dental office carrying that heavy box, I was attracted to her. I pursued her without getting to really know her first. That's my fault."

"If you say so," Jonetta shrugged. "Be that as it may, son, don't go beating yourself up about all of this. The worst part is over. Now we can all move forward without *that* hanging over our heads. You are my greatest gift late in life. You've given me a reason to fight for my health and stick around a little longer. We have a lot of catching up to do."

"Why are you so harsh on your daughters?" Bishon asked, dismissing her adoration for him. Somebody had to ask, might as well have been the newcomer.

Jonetta jerked her neck. Here she was having an endearing moment with him and he wanted to ruin it by questioning her. "You seem to be in a foul mood today. Don't go ruining our special time together."

"Maybe you're not aware of how you treat them sometimes. I've watched you interact with them and you're quite critical of all three of them. They are only humans who make mistakes… just like I did. Trust me, I make a lot of mistakes. But you act like they are a thorn in your side when they make mistakes."

"Well, they are!" Jonetta declared.

Bishon's mouth flew open. He couldn't believe his ears. His mother, Barbara, would never dream of being so critical of him. *So these are your true colors, huh?* "Come on, now. That's not fair," Bishon said, and began pacing the floor. "They didn't ask to be born and neither did I! Did you even want me?" Bishon finally asked. He hated being vulnerable, but he had no choice if he wanted answers.

"Yes," Jonetta replied, reaching for his hand. "Come sit down."

Bishon exhaled sharply and took a seat again. "I'm listening."

"It was me and you on that long bus ride to Chicago. It was me and you cleaning and washing in that big old house. It was me and you eating late at night. It was me and you sleeping and dreaming of a better life. All I had was you…inside of me. I talked to you every single day. When I sang, you would just be flipping around and kicking inside of me. You gave me great joy in a horrible situation.

I couldn't wait to see your face, but I never had the chance. I didn't even get to hold you. My aunts told me that you died and that was that."

"Sounds like you were really lonely when you moved here," Bishon acknowledge her pain. "Norman told me that last year at Thanksgiving, you revealed what happened to you and the work your great aunts had you doing in that house. That must've been an awful secret to keep for decades," Bishon said searching her face. "I'm sorry."

Jonetta exhaled and sat quiet for a moment. "I didn't share everything because I don't like to talk about it. Who wants to know that their mother used to be a prostitute? But even at Thanksgiving, I still didn't know that you were alive and well. Isn't that something?"

"What a difference nine months can make, huh?"

"No kidding. Life or death can happen easily in nine months. But I'm so glad it is life this time. We've had enough of death."

"Who is my father?" Bishon asked readily.

Jonetta released his hand and swallowed hard. "Son, I'm so tired. All of this talking has worn me out. Can you make some tea for me?"

"No! I need answers."

"Bishon! What has gotten into you today?" For a split second, the anger in his face reminded Jonetta so much of his father, Paul King.

"Jonetta, I swear! You're so good at redirecting the conversation. I'm beginning feel like you're just using me to mend this family!" Bishon hissed.

"So now I've been reduced to Jonetta instead of Mama?"

Bishon threw his hands in the air. "I rest my case! Do you even genuinely care about me as a person?"

"Of course! You're my son!"

"Then why won't you answer my question?"

"Because he raped me!"

Chapter 25

It was a new day, and Phyllis finally felt refreshed. Her nights had been restless over the past few weeks thanks to everyone's drama. Dawn's abortion had been weighing heavy on her heart. After Jonetta had forced her to get an abortion as a teenager, Phyllis had difficulty trying to get pregnant with her husband. Now she had regrets about driving Dawn to the abortion clinic.

With that looming guilt on her mind, Jonetta's recovery was also on the forefront of her mind. Will she ever be the same? Her mind seemed to be still sharp, but not her body. Colette's court case was a disaster and she just might lose custody of her children. Owen was making this much harder than it had to be. It was personal. Bishon was inserting himself in their lives, whether they wanted him around or not. All of it had taken a toll her spirit, but today she felt much better.

Usually, after the school bus picked up the twins, she didn't get back in the bed, but today she needed that extra snuggle. There were so many things on her To-Do list, but before she emerged from her warm bed to tend to her neglected house chores, she grabbed the remote to the television, then thought better of it. She remembered all she had to do was talk out loud.

"Alexa, turn to *Good Morning America*." Phyllis smiled as the smart device obeyed her commands. Damien was totally against having it in the house because he was convinced that the government was listening, but the Cyber Monday sale was too good to pass up. Even he took advantage of it sometimes when he wanted the lights off or needed to help the girls with homework. It came in handy, he just didn't want to admit it.

Awww man! Phyllis frowned when she didn't see Robin Roberts at the desk with her colleagues. She was the only reason Phyllis still tuned into the show. "Alexa, turn to NBC *Today*." If Phyllis couldn't have Robin, she always settled for Hoda Kotb.

Both channels were discussing Labor Day weekend must-haves meats and veggies on the grill. Looking at all that food gave Phyllis an idea about her afternoon cooking show. She would show her viewers how to achieve making great dishes without the grill for Labor Day.

Phyllis was excited as the ideas swirled in her head. Chicken wing skewers stacked with bell peppers, onions, and pineapples. Oh and she couldn't forget about ground turkey baked beans with barbeque sauce. All of this could be made on the stove and in the oven and she was about to show her viewers just how to achieve it by making it taste like it came off the grill with her special mesquite dry rub.

"Alexa, turn the T.V. off." Phyllis tossed the comforter to Damien's side of the bed, slid her feet inside of her pink fuzzy slippers and headed downstairs. The moment she hit the top of the landing, she smelled bacon and coffee brewing. *What the hell?*

"Damien? Why aren't you at work?"

"Well, good morning to you, too!" He planted a kiss on her cheek and handed her a cup of coffee. "I whipped up some cheesy eggs and finally used the air fryer for some bacon. It came out perfect!"

Phyllis didn't say thank you, she didn't smile and she didn't return the kiss. She was annoyed by his presence in her kitchen where she made magic happen. He was supposed to be at work today. She sipped her cup of coffee and was grateful that it was perfect. *One less thing to fuss about.*

"I thought I heard you leave out this morning?"

"You did. I ran to the store to grab a few items to make breakfast," Damien smiled. "Let me fix your plate."

"What do you have up your sleeve?" Phyllis raised her eyebrow suspiciously.

"Nothing. I just needed a mental health day, you feel me?"

"No, I don't 'feel' you. Are you getting paid for this 'mental health day'?"

"Of course!" Damien scoffed. "Don't ever worry about that, babe. All the money is accounted for safe in the bank. My gambling days are over, remember? I just needed a break from the hustle and bustle. Lucky for you, now you don't have to cook breakfast for yourself. I got you!"

Phyllis scanned the kitchen to see the eggs were still left out. *Salmonella poisoning.* Three pots were still on the stove. *Those should be soaking.* Dishes were in the sink and the countertop had food splatter and crumbs everywhere. *Yeah, lucky for me. More cleaning up behind you before I go live.*

"Well, looks like you have some cleaning to do before my food segment on Facebook live." Phyllis knew that topic was a sore spot for him, but mentioned it anyway to send a message.

"Yeah, I'll clean it all up before you go live. Just have a seat and eat." Damien placed her plate of food right in front of her and planted another kiss on her forehead.

"Don't mind if I do." Phyllis ate a forkful of eggs and closed her eyes. She had loved his eggs from the moment he made breakfast for her the very first time she spent the night at his apartment. He had been making them the same way for over ten years now.

"So is everyone going to avoid your brother like the plague? Or act like adults and get to know him?" Damien asked out of the blue.

"Half-brother," Phyllis reminded him, rolling her eyes. "Where is this coming from?"

"Labor Day is coming up and we always barbeque," Damien replied, scooping eggs on his plate.

"And?" Phyllis probed, nibbling on bacon.

"Well, is he part of the family invitation or not?"

Phyllis sat stiff as a board in her chair and dropped her fork. She had just lost her appetite. "You know what, Damien? I've had a lot on my plate lately with my family. When I think of family, Bishon is not a thought in my mind. He's the furthest thing from it. Family is considered a group of people who have been through life with you on a rollercoaster, held your hand, wiped your tears, shared your joys and dusted you off when you've been beat down by life. That's family to me and he was not part of it! Maybe that's harsh of me. So what? I'm human. I'm not about to overextend myself to embrace him. He's a complete stranger as far as I'm concerned. Clearly, Mama wants him around…permanently. That's fine. That's her child. But when it comes to extending invitations to Bishon, it won't be coming from me."

Back in the guest room, Dawn stretched across the bed and mindlessly scrolled through her Instagram. She immediately stopped when she saw a photo of the cast of *The Haves and Have Nots* on Vine's page. Yes, she still followed him, but never liked on any of the pics since their breakup. She didn't want to give him the satisfaction of ever thinking they could even be friends. Now, looking at his smile jump from the picture, she regretted treating him as if he had cheated on her. All he wanted was to take their relationship to the next level. He wanted her to be his wife. That's it. But she ran from that lifestyle right into Raffi and Chena's home, playing the wife instead of actually being one.

Mama was right! I would've looked really good on his arm. She looked at the photo closer to see if she could pick up any vibes with him and any of the female cast members. Nope. It looked like a bunch of professional coworkers taking a group photo on set. Innocent. *What do you have to lose?* Dawn double clicked the photo, watched the heart popup and smiled.

A knock on the door startled her. "Come in," she said sitting upright.

"Hey, sis," Phyllis said softly. "How are you feeling?"

"Ehhh, so-so. I keep getting cramps."

"Are you taking your meds?"

Dawn nodded. "Yeah, but I may need something holistic, like CBD oil."

"How are you gonna get some CBD oil?"

"No worries. It's not illegal." Dawn waved her off.

Phyllis gave her a side-eye, but decided not to pursue that conversation. She had another issue that needed her full attention.

"Can you connect to Facebook?"

"I was just on Instagram, but let me check," Dawn said and pulled up the app on her iPhone. "Yeah, I'm good."

"I can't connect and I need to go live in an hour!" Phyllis exclaimed. "Well, let me know if you need anything. I need to figure this mess out."

Phyllis returned to the kitchen only to find Damien lingering. *Oh my God! I wish he'd just disappear if he can't be useful.*

"Babe, I'm sorry if I upset you," Damien began. "It's just that Bishon seems like a cool dude. I wanna get to know him."

Phyllis waved him off. "I've got bigger fish to fry, babe."

"What happened now?"

"There's something wrong with my account!" Phyllis fumed.

"Your bank account?" Damien asked.

"No, my Facebook account."

"Oh," he replied and waved her off.

Phyllis placed her hand on her hip out of frustration. "It may not seem like a crisis to you, but I need to go live in thirty minutes and I cannot log on!"

"Try checking your notifications or messages," Damien suggested. "That happened to my boy before and come to find out, he was in jail."

"What do you mean 'jail'?"

"Facebook will shut your page down or limit your access if you've violated their policy or somebody snitched on you for posting...well you know… nudes or porn. It's called Facebook jail." Damien explained with a chuckle.

"Snitched on me? Violated their policy? What in the world? I didn't commit either of those crimes." Phyllis frantically checked her inbox messages. "Holy shit! I'm in Facebook jail."

"Told ya!" Damien said, sipping on orange juice. He peered over her shoulder to read the message, but couldn't get a good look. "Well, what does it say exactly?"

Phyllis slumped her shoulders and exhaled. "Someone reported me for child abuse on my last video."

"What the hell!?" Damien shrieked. "What happened on the last live post you made?"

"I popped the twins on the hand for using my utensils," Phyllis began to explain with concern etched in her face. "But…but that's *not* abuse. Oh, my God. This could get ugly. What if the Department of Child and Family Services show up at our door?"

"That's it! No more of this going live on Facebook crap!" Damien slammed his glass on the kitchen counter. "Ever since you've been doing this…this cooking show or whatever, it's been nothing but trouble for us!"

"Trouble? There hasn't been any trouble stemming from my cooking show, what are you talking about?" Phyllis asked defensively.

"Well, for starters, I don't like people having access to what my house looks like, but now everyone knows. Secondly, you put me on Facebook live one time and my inbox blew up!" Damien replied.

"Blew up?" Phyllis frowned.

"Are you a parakeet today? Yes! It blew up! All types of women were flooding my inbox with messages, sending me pics…unsolicited pics! They were disrespectfully flirting with me and downright bold as hell telling me what they wanted to do with me. Nobody knew who the hell I was until you put me on the spot, filming me without my consent."

"Oh, really?" Phyllis folded her arms across her chest. "That must've really been awful for you, huh? And what was your response to all of these women who were flirting with you?"

"Whatever! My point is, enough is enough!" Damien snapped, slamming his fist on the kitchen counter. "Now look what we have to deal with because of *your* cooking show. This is exactly why I'm against strangers coming into my house for this cooking class! I swear to God if DCFS shows up I'm going to snap the hell off!"

Phyllis ignored his tantrum and continued reading her messages. There was another one from the corporate office explaining why her show was canceled before it even got started. "Well, it looks like you'll get your wish," Phyllis said somberly. "The offer has been rescinded."

Chapter 26

After a month home from the hospital, Jonetta was recovering well and her physical therapy sessions were the extra push she needed to feel whole again. She was ready to tackle any unfinished business prior to her stroke until Colette called several times asking her to help with Georgia's belongings. What Colette didn't realize was the last place Jonetta needed to be was in that house, where she had killed her sister.

It was weighing heavy on Jonetta at the funeral, but since she'd been home recovering from her stroke, she tucked those thoughts away during her healing. Now she had no choice but to face the demons waiting for her because Norman had convinced her that spending time with Colette and the grandchildren would improve her spirits.

"I think getting out of this house will do your soul some good," Norman suggested. "Besides, Colette is really going through a hard time with the custody case."

"I'd rather burn the house to the ground than step foot in it."

"She needs her Mama."

"They all do, especially Bishon," Jonetta remarked.

"But right now, we're talking about Colette. Come on, I'll drive you over there. I'll keep the grandkids entertained while you and Colette organize things."

On the late afternoon drive, Jonetta had an upset stomach. Norman had sworn it was due to the cheesy potatoes that he made for breakfast, but Jonetta knew otherwise. She had secretly hoped that they could at least catch a flat tire along the way, but no such luck. They glided along in the burgundy Lincoln Town Car, cruising as the dusties played on the radio. The moment they pulled up to *that* house that held so many awful memories, so much shame and guilt, Jonetta knew this was a bad idea.

Norman opened the passenger side door, reached out his hand to help her out and she inhaled sharply. *Why did I let you talk me into this?* She took a moment to gather her thoughts, holding onto her purse.

"Netta?" Norman said, bending down to peer into the car. "You coming out?"

"We're here now," Jonetta responded dryly. She retreated from the passenger seat slowly and finally exhaled. The last thing she wanted to do was be inside that house. Every time she thought about her sister, Georgia, a vision of her limp body in the chair would flash in her mind. It was vivid. It was real. It was her fault.

"Grandma!" Lydia squealed running out the front door. Before Jonetta knew it, all three of her grandchildren were wrapped around her body.

"Come on kids, let's go inside," Norman said, eyeing Jonetta. He could tell something was off and regretted bringing her. "Listen, we don't have to stay long, okay?"

"I told you that I didn't want to come at all," Jonetta replied through clenched teeth.

Once inside, Colette was in the kitchen cleaning. That's the last place Jonetta wanted to be sitting. She looked at the refrigerator where the "special tea" had been the ruin of Georgia. Jonetta inhaled sharply again and cleared her throat.

"Well, where do we begin?"

"Hi Mama," Colette said, searching her face. "Are you alright? You look kinda pale."

Jonetta touched her face and replied, "Let's just get this over with before I get too tired."

"Hi Dad!" Colette greeted him with a hug.

"Hey, sweetheart," Norman replied, planting a kiss on her cheek.

"Thanks for bringing Mama today. I hope the kids run you raggedy like they do me!" Colette giggled, patted him on the shoulder and escorted Jonetta upstairs.

Jonetta climbed the stairs slowly, not because her body couldn't manage, she just didn't want to manage her emotions. *I'm too old for this shit.* When she looked around Georgia's room, she realized how small it was, yet it was packed with clothes, books, shoes, magazines and boxes of God-knows-what.

"It's overwhelming, I know," Colette said. "This is just her dressing room, not where she slept."

Jonetta raised her eyebrows. "Georgia was always 'Miss High Society' even when we were kids."

"I adored her fashion sense. Unfortunately, I can't fit any of her clothes," Colette rambled on. She held up a pink, silk blouse, brought it close to her nose and inhaled. "And she always wore the most feminine perfume. You wanna smell it?"

Jonetta frowned and shook her head. "I don't even want to be here. It's way too bad many memories. Don't you think this house is way too big for you to handle?"

Colette stopped folding clothes to ponder that notion. "No, not really. The kids need the room to grow and the yard is the perfect place for them to play instead of the park. Why?"

"If you could get your act together, I wouldn't have to deal with this house at all!" Jonetta said fiercely. She had been in a foul mood since she crossed the threshold.

"Mama, I don't have another place to go right now. What are you gonna do, sell the house and have your grandkids out on the street just so you can be rid of your demons?" Colette took her frustrations out on the laundry, forcefully stuffing a stack of shirts into the dresser drawer. "Besides, you can't sell the house right now because Owen is talking about moving in here part-time. He doesn't want to fight with me in the courts. He'd rather us to just be a family again." She mumbled partly in disbelief she just let that slip.

"What did you say?" Jonetta stopped sorting through her sister's clothing, squinted her eyes to get a good look at her daughter. She heard exactly what Colette mumbled and she didn't miss the doubt in her voice either.

Colette shrugged, kept her eyes focused on the laundry and replied, "He stopped by the other night and basically told me that he wanted us to be a family again. If I agreed, he would drop the case for full custody. But if I refused, he'd ask the judge just to take Cornell to live with him because apparently Shante doesn't want five kids to take care of in her house." She slowly lifted her eyes to meet her mother's and immediately regretted saying anything at all.

"What the hell?" Jonetta sprang to her feet, dropping a few items of clothes from her lap and a few envelopes slid across the floor unnoticed in her rage. "Take Cornell? That ignorant, arrogant, sack of shit! *You* have custody of the kids, Colette! The cards are in your hands!"

"Mama, please sit down. You're going to work yourself up," Colette said concerned. *If she has a setback it'll be all of my fault.*

Jonetta took a deep breath and continued, "Owen can't give *you* an ultimatum when he's the one who screwed up in your marriage… or your relationship… or whatever! I know you're not about to fall for his manipulative ways! I wish he would try to take Cornell from you! It'll be over my damn dead body!" Jonetta snarled as her arms went flailing in the air.

"Mama, please calm down. You're not out of the woods from that stroke." Colette slowly approached her mother, touching her shoulder softly.

Jonetta snatched away, knitting her brows together. "You're clearly trying to give me another one!" Her nostrils flared as her chest heaved.

Colette shook her head vehemently. "No, Mama. I'm just trying to keep the peace with that man and have him change his full custody plea to visitation only."

Jonetta pointed her slender, wrinkled finger at Colette and continued, "Here you go again, setting yourself on fire trying to keep other people warm! When will you ever learn?"

"Well, what am I supposed to do when he threatens me with taking away my son if I don't let him move in?" Colette threw her hands in the air. "I certainly won't let him take Cornell to live over there with that whore, Shante, and their new son. It'll be over *my* dead body, Mama!"

Jonetta placed her hand over her face and exhaled. "Since he's such a good father figure, did you even bother to ask him why he's trying to leave that other woman and *his* son? Did you bother to ask how is it that he has options to either live with you *and* her?"

Colette didn't think about it that way. All she heard was, he would drop the full custody case. She swallowed hard and frowned, but didn't answer her mother.

"Owen is probably over there pissing her off and just needs a place to stay. That's the only reason he would give such a ridiculous ultimatum like that! He's in no position to be a positive father figure to Cornell. He's a con artist with a silver tongue. Don't be stupid! I swear, if I find out that he's living in this house, I'll put the house on the market regardless if you have a place to live!"

"Wow! I'm not stupid, Mama! That's pretty cold of you to say. I bet you'd never talk to Bishon like that!" Colette fumed, slamming the dresser drawer shut. "I told him what he needed to hear that night. I told him that I agreed with it because I could see that he was high and I didn't want to get in a fight."

"So you slept with him instead!" Jonetta grunted, gave her daughter a side eye and pursed her lips. She knew all too well what it took to calm a man down when he was drunk or high. *This damn girl is sleeping with the enemy. I swear to God if she gets pregnant again, I'm going to strangle her!* Jonetta shook her head and took a seat on the edge of the bed. Remembering what her physical therapist told her about remaining calm, she inhaled a slow deep breath, held it for three seconds and exhaled.

"No… I … we didn't," Colette lied

Jonetta waved her off. "So now what?"

Colette shrugged her shoulders and began to pick up the clothes and envelopes from the floor. "Like I said, I'm not stupid. I mean… of course, I want my family to be together, but a life with Owen is nothing but chaos. I'm so over that life, especially in front of my kids. It's not healthy for any of us."

"Well, that's a relief to hear you say that." Jonetta remarked, smoothing the fabric of her slacks. "I'll let your father know that Owen is threatening to kidnap his only grandson."

Colette chuckled. "Don't go getting Dad involved in my mess, please. Besides, what's he gonna do about it?"

"Don't underestimate your father and his connections. I didn't marry a punk." Jonetta winked, then added, "Owen didn't get a black eye and broken arm two summers ago on the basketball court by accident."

Colette jerked her neck, surprised at that news.

Jonetta raised her eyebrows and nodded. "That's right! Your father doesn't appreciate anyone putting their hands on any of his precious jewels. And that goes for his grandchildren, too."

Colette eyed her mother, slowed her steps as a tingling sensation shot through her body. She certainly had underestimated her father.

"Dad was responsible for that? Owen was hurt pretty bad from that fight."

"Yeah, and so were you." Jonetta countered.

Colette swallowed hard as she recalled how Owen slapped her so hard that she did a 180-degree spin, landing on their faux wood coffee table with a busted lip and broken nose. She shuddered remembering how her bruised face and blood shot eyes kept her inside the house all summer. Now, knowing that her father was responsible for getting Owen roughed up, she felt loved, important, and cared for which were all new emotions for her. A wide smile spread across her flushed face then suddenly, she remembered at the funeral that her father had mentioned that there was so much she didn't know about him, including the fact that he had been married before.

Thanks to all the commotion when Jonetta passed out in the parking lot, rushing to the hospital, dealing with the kids, praying feverishly that her mother would wake up and hoping when she did that she wouldn't be physically deformed from the stroke, that she'd forgotten all about that little golden nugget that her dad dropped in her lap. Colette contemplated mentioning it to her mother now, but instead made a mental note to bring that up in conversation the next time she spoke to her father.

Colette placed the envelopes on the nightstand and shook out two blouses and a pair of slacks. The fragrance of Georgia's perfume wafted over them. She held the clothes close to her chest, closed her eyes and inhaled again. "Gosh, I truly miss Aunt Georgia." Colette released a nostalgic sigh. "She was such a beautiful person, inside and out."

Jonetta looked away quickly, bowed her head as her stomach did a somersault. Fearing that skeleton bones would fall out of her mouth, she nodded in agreement, picked at her cuticles and kept her mouth closed. There were way too many emotions swirling inside of her to form a sentence. She had already let one cat out of the bag for the day and that was one too many.

"Anyway, Mama... ummm… Sorry, I didn't mean to upset you."

Jonetta waved her hand, "No, don't worry about it. I'm glad you shared that with me."

"I'm gonna start dinner for the kids." Colette leaned down, planted a kiss on Jonetta's cheek and closed the bedroom door behind her.

Jonetta sat stiff as a statue for a minute as her thoughts riddled her with guilt. Finally, she flicked away tears that were welling up and swallowed the thick lump growing in her throat. *I'll take that sin to my grave.*

As she smoothed the edges of her hair, guiding them up towards her neat bun, her eyes landed on the stack of envelopes that Colette placed on the nightstand. The envelopes were unopened with outdated stamps she recognized from at least twenty years ago or more. Her eyes grew wide when she saw *J. Henderson* scribbled on the front. She snatched the pile sorting through them one-by-one; they all were addressed to her in both her maiden and married names. The date stamps varied from the 60's through the 80's from Pennsylvania. *Who are these from?* She flipped an envelope over to the front and in scribbled writing it read: *Ernestine Henderson*. Her mother.

Chapter 27

Bishon paced his living room floor, back and forth, studying the grooves etched in the grey toned wood. The glass of Bulleit Rye Whiskey was supposed to do the trick, but it wasn't. His nerves were bad. He knocked back another gulp hoping the liquor would do its job in the next few minutes. Beads of sweat formed on his forehead and he allowed them to linger as his thoughts traveled back a few days.

He hadn't planned on raising his voice at Jonetta; he just wanted answers. All that he knew was that Jonetta had been prostituted, but Norman rescued her somehow. None of that explained how his existence ever came about though. He was alive, loved, cared for and adored by his adoptive parents, true enough, but there was more to him and he wanted to know, deserved to know more.

His personal life was unraveling and spilling over into his professional life. It was unfamiliar territory. He dropped to the floor and immediately began push-ups. With every pump he saw Dawn's face. Pump 10. Dawn smiling. Pump 15. Dawn laughing. Pump 20. Dawn's veins protruding from her neck when she climaxed. Pump 25. Dawn twirling her hair. By the time he reached pushup number 50, he wanted to vomit. Now, stretched out across the floor with beads of sweat forming across his forehead, he tried to catch his breath. He covered his face with his hands and exhaled.

"She is your SISTER!" he felt the vibration of his voice through his body. Bishon rolled to his side and curled up in a fetal position. Before he could let out another cry, his phone rang. It was

Dawn's ring tone. He sprang to his feet, dashed towards the kitchen counter where he last placed it and answered as normal as he could.

"Hello?"

There was a moment of silence.

"I thought that I would hear from you by now," Dawn began.

"I was waiting for the right time to call you," Bishon explained.

"The 'right time' is when you *make* time," Dawn countered.

Another moment of awkward silence passed.

"I'm sorry," Bishon exhaled. "How are you feeling?"

Dawn sighed. "Like life just kicked my ass."

"I'm sorry," Bishon apologized again.

"Don't go beating yourself up. It takes two to tango, ya know? Besides, I'm glad it's over. I can move on with my life. We both can have a fresh start."

"No, I'm not going to downplay what you just went through alone."

"I wasn't alone. Phyllis was with me."

"I should've been there," Bishon replied riddled with guilt. "I'm not going to put on a brave face about any of this, Dawn. This is my first time at this rodeo and it doesn't feel good. I want to talk to you, comfort you, see you, but…"

"I'm on my way."

***

Tears. She was fresh out of them. She had no time for them. Not this time around. Dawn was ready to do things her way. The longing to be held, comforted and caressed was long overdue. She had toiled with the idea of getting what she needed from Raffi, but she knew that would come with a hefty cost: harassment. Bishon was a much better choice. Besides, they had a lot to talk about. How were they going to muddle through life as siblings knowing full well they still had feelings for one another?

Time to face some demons. Dawn moisturized her skin with Shea butter as soon as she stepped out the shower. She glided her hands around her breasts in a circular motion stimulating her nipples. Out of curiosity, she squeezed them and gasped when she saw white liquid appear. "What the hell?" She cupped her breasts and squeezed again to see if more would escape, it did. She had made a mental note to make a follow-up appointment with a doctor.

Dawn looked at herself in the mirror and frowned. Her body in perfect shape, per usual, but her lower abdomen had a little pouch. "You've got to go and so does this milk." Thanks to her career in the fashion and modeling industry, her concern was always her outer appearance, but it was the inside that needed a lot of work.

At 33-years-old, she had just had her first abortion, not that she ever thought she was exempt from it. Dawn knew that she had a reckless sex life, yet and still she was in shock and drowning in guilt. Unlike Bishon, she was good at putting on a brave face, but no matter how she tried to mask her true feelings, she felt awful about her decision. She needed someone to tell her it wasn't her fault. She needed someone to tell her that she did the right thing. She needed Bishon.

Dawn chose an army fatigue tank top dress to wear with flip flops and tossed her hair up in a floppy bun. She didn't want to come across to Bishon as having it all together after an abortion because she didn't. So she kept it simple.

"I'll be back, sis." Dawn said descending down the stairs. She didn't know if Phyllis heard her or not, but the twins did.

"Where are you going Aunty Dawn?" Serena asked.

"Can we come, too?" Sabrina chimed in.

Dawn patted them both on the head, threw on her shades and gave them a kiss good-bye on the cheeks. "Tell your mommy that I'll be back later."

The drive to Bishon's condo was always refreshing down Lake Shore Drive. It wasn't as humid as it could have been in Chicago and she was thankful. The sky was clear blue and it invited her to open the moon roof and welcome the end-of-summer breeze. A smile crept across her face when she heard Lizzo play over the speakers. She turned up the volume, cruising the rest of the way. No traffic, just her, Lizzo and the waves crashing on the rocks down Lake Shore Drive. *Why couldn't life be this way all the time?*

Once she pulled into her assigned guest parking space, she fumbled around in her purse looking for her gummy bears. Smoking a joint was out of the question because she didn't want to smell like she had just been in a session and Bishon hated when she smoked. She tore into the bag, stuffing two of the gummy bears in her mouth at once. She continued to munch on them until they became moist and gooey. She flipped the sun visor down to get a good look at herself.

"I guess you look how you feel, huh?" Dawn chuckled. "You'll feel better once these babies kick in."

When Bishon opened the door his cologne wafted in her direction, causing a tingle between her legs. *He's wearing that cologne that I love on him. What the hell? Is he trying to seduce me?*

"Hey, come on in," Bishon said, stepping aside.

"No hug?"

Bishon closed the door and awkwardly embraced Dawn.

"You smell good."

"Thanks," Bishon said, darting his eyes away. He purposely wore that cologne to entice her, but why? He knew their truth now. They were siblings, but he still had a desire to please her. "Would you like anything to drink or eat?"

Dawn shook her head no as she walked towards the living room windows that went from floor to ceiling. "I'm good." She loved his view of the city. The McCormick Place and the lake front both shimmered in the sunlight, looking like new money. On Saturdays residents on his side of the building could see the fireworks display at Navy Pier.

From across the room, propped up against the island, Bishon watched her in her own world, his face full of desire. The gummy bears were effectively working through Dawn's system now. She hummed out of key, mindlessly twirling loose strands of her hair. "I could stand here forever just watching the world keep busy. Don't ever move from this condo, Bishon. I'm gonna need this view in my life."

"Okay," Bishon chuckled. "What type of meds did they give you?"

Dawn spun around, studied his face for a moment then slid down the glass window with a thud. "Vicodin, of course."

"Are you alright?" Bishon asked, rushing to help her off the wooden floor. "Did you take any meds before you left the house?"

Dawn shook her head no and waved him off when he extended his hand to her. "I'm fine down here. Sit with me."

"On the floor?"

"Yeah! Didn't the maid come this week?"

Bishon nodded his head and obliged her request. They both sat Indian style on the floor facing one another, but with enough space between them. He touched her knee gently and she squeezed his hand in return.

"I'm here," he said softly. "Whatever you need, I'm here."

Dawn leaned forward and replied, "You can't give me what I need."

"What do you mean by that?" Bishon asked defensively. "I've always been here for you, Dawn. Nothing about my availability to you will change. I was just giving you some space."

"I don't need 'space' and you know that," Dawn said, poking the tip of his nose.

"Just tell me what you need," Bishon replied desperately.

Dawn unfolded her legs, crawled on all fours towards him and laid her head in his lap. She started humming again as if the radio was playing her favorite tune on repeat. Bishon caressed the side of her face gently and she hugged his legs like she never wanted to let go.

Suddenly she popped her head up as if she forgot to do something.

"Did you know that I have milk?"

"What?" Bishon asked, baffled.

Dawn sat upright, slid her arms out of her tank top dress, pulled it down to expose her perfectly shaped B-cup breasts and began massaging them until milk excreted. "See it coming out?"

Bishon raised his brows in awe and swallowed hard. His face flushed with embarrassment as he began to feel swelling in his pants. He was aroused by the very sight of her, especially now with her breasts fully exposed. He remained silent while he tried to steady his breathing, heart rate and control his thoughts at the same time. *Relax dude. There's no way it's gonna happen. She's your sister.*

"Nobody told me that I would have milk…afterwards," Dawn said in disbelief as she smeared the wetness on her nipples and pulled up her dress.

Bishon decided stand up just in case she wanted to lie in his lap again, but immediately regretted it when Dawn's expression changed.

"Is that for me?" she grinned and knelt in front of him in complete submission. The look on her face was full of desire and lust. She bit her bottom lip and slowly glided her hands up his legs until she almost touched his erect member.

"We can't," Bishon said, grabbing her hands.

"We can't," Dawn repeated, staring directly into his eyes.

"I want to," he admitted, pulling Dawn to her feet.

"Me too," Dawn replied, pressing her pelvis against his and kissing his neck.

Oh, shit! That feels good, Bishon thought.

Dawn walked to the island, poured out a shot of whiskey and took it to the head. She flinched as it stung going down. "I should go," Dawn said, walking towards the door.

"I don't want you to go," Bishon said, grabbing her hand and gently pulling her closer to him. He ran his fingers through her curls and sighed. *To hell with it.* Bishon led her to his bedroom and closed the door.

Chapter 28

Jonetta was settled comfortably in her chair, taking a moment to at least read half of the unopened letters from her mother that she found in a stack of Georgia's belongings. Her handwriting, misspellings and sentence structure was a clear indication that she lacked proper education. It took several attempts for Jonetta just to get through one letter. But with the help of her reading glasses, she finally deciphered exactly what her mother was conveying and it became a bit easier to interpret.

An hour had past when Jonetta realized that most of the letters consisted of local and family updates, nothing really profound. *Why did Georgia hold onto these letters all these years? They are clearly mine!* She pondered. Jonetta removed her reading glasses and rubbed her eyes gently. They had begun to burn from all the straining and squinting she had to do just to make sense of the letters. She gathered the stack of envelopes and sifted through them to organize them neatly when she noticed a manila envelope folded in half. It was thin, but had legible handwriting on it. Jonetta's fingers fumbled trying to find the perfect corner to slide the letter opener underneath. She couldn't open the envelope fast enough. "Dammit!" she yelped. In her haste, she got a paper cut. She sucked her middle finger before the blood could appear and continued to open the envelope. At first sight it appeared to be a legal document of sorts. Placing her reading glasses back on to get a better look, she saw that it was Georgia's Last Will and Testament.

Before Jonetta could get a look at the details, Norman appeared. "Is everything alright? I thought I heard you yell."

"Just a stupid paper cut," she mumbled still fixated on the document.

"Is it deep?" he asked, leaning in to get a closer look. Jonetta was so engrossed in what Georgia had left behind in her will that she tuned him out. The will listed clothing, furs, jewelry, bank accounts and her car and land back in Pennsylvania. *Land?*

"You're bleeding all over whatever you're reading!"

Norman screeched, heading for the restroom for tissue and bandages.

Jonetta winced when she saw the blood stains on the document. “Dammit!” she said again angrier about the document being ruined than her pain. “I’m alright, Norman.”

“Here,” he said handing her a box of tissue and bandages. He took the papers from her and placed it on the table. “What’s got all of your attention?”

“While I was helping Colette sort through Georgia’s things, a stack of envelopes fell from God knows where because the room is so cluttered,” Jonetta explained, wrapping her finger with tissue. She then carefully tore the thin paper from the bandage and wrapped it around her finger. “Mostly, they were letters from my mother written to me over the span of two decades. For the life of me, I have no idea why Georgia never gave them to me.”

“That’s odd,” Norman said and took a seat on the sofa.

“I agree. Then I just noticed that envelope a few moments ago,” Jonetta said nodding her head towards the will. “That’s Georgia’s will.”

“No kidding?” Norman leaned over to grab the papers. He carefully held the corners that didn’t have blood on it and began reading it, raising his brows and grunting.

Jonetta cringed at the sight of her blood on the paper and glanced at her bandaged finger. Paper cuts always seemed to hurt the most, as tiny as they were, the pain was undeniable. Her finger began to throb mainly because she wrapped the bandage too tight. She turned her attention to Norman, who was making grunting sounds the more he read the will. Jonetta began to get annoyed because he got further along than she did reading.

“If you don’t mind?” she said extending her hand.

“Can I finish reading it for myself?”

“Did you see this part about land back in Pennsylvania?”

“Yes. Now can I finish reading it?”

Norman handed the papers to her and leaned back on the sofa. He pondered Jonetta and Georgia’s peculiar relationship as sisters. As he thought more about it, their whole family dynamic was strange. Jonetta had three brothers that she never spoke about as if they didn’t exist. Georgia was the only one she had kept in touch with over the years, yet she never gave a stack of letter from their mother to Jonetta. He shook his head and waved his thoughts away.

"Well, we need a lawyer to take a look at the will and then go from there."

Jonetta grunted in agreement as she continued to read Georgia's will. "It says here that she wanted to leave her Mercedes to Colette." She snatched off her reading glasses and plopped them in her lap.

"Really? But Dawn had claimed that car even while Georgia was alive," Norman replied, rubbing his chin. "What date is on the will?"

"Maybe we should keep this to ourselves and let things just sort themselves out," Jonetta said, folding the paper in half.

"Things just don't get sorted out on their own, Netta. That's way of thinking is a recipe for how to ignite confusion and keep bullshit going! That's why this family is so divided now."

"No bullshit will be started if you just keep quiet about it!"

Norman waved her off. "You and your secrets."

"Who doesn't have secrets? And we're not a family divided. We're simply going through growing pains with Bishon. But everything will work itself out. You'll see."

Norman shook his head. He didn't have it in him to argue with her today. He slowly rose from the sofa to head to the patio for some fresh air. "Well, I'm staying out of it."

"I'm going to look into this little piece of land that my Mama left behind for me." Jonetta nodded her head in absolution, ignoring his last comment.

"From what I just read, she didn't leave it to just you. The property was left to all of the siblings. Do you know how to contact your brothers? When was the last time you spoke to them?" He couldn't help it. Jonetta was really getting underneath his skin. He wanted her to realize that there was a bigger picture that she should consider.

"Norman!" Jonetta fumed. "I truly wish you'd shut the hell up!"

Her wish was granted when he immediately exited the room.

In the late afternoon, Jonetta tried her best to rest her eyes, but the more she thought about how Georgia had kept the letters from her all these years, she didn't feel so bad about accidentally poisoning her after all. *I would've never discovered these letters from my mother otherwise,* she reasoned. Reflecting on her death also triggered memories of Mr. Lucky, Big Louie, Georgia, Aunt Betty Lou and Aunt Adell. They had all flashed before her eyes as she was trying to rest. Jonetta had played a hand in each of their demise in some way. Was she a murderer? Did she have a murderous soul? No. She was simply a victim of her own circumstance…at least that's what she had told herself.

Not soon after her mind finally stopped tormenting her, the doorbell rang. Jonetta exhaled sharply, placing her right hand over her eyes. *I'm not in the mood for company. As soon as I recover completely from this stroke, I need to move out of here.* She shut off her grumbling thoughts and tried to listen closely to the muffled voices. *It's a man.* She listened intently again to determine if she knew the voice, but she couldn't make it out.

Moments later a knock on the door startled her. *For God's sakes!* She clutched her oversized t-shirt, glanced at her appearance and decided that she was decent enough.

"Come in."

"Helloooo," Bishon said, peeking his head in the door. "Are you decent?"

"Bishon! What a nice surprise!" Jonetta exclaimed, extending her arms for a welcoming hug. *I need to learn how to recognize my own son's voice.*

Bishon obliged and welcomed her warm embrace.

"What happened to your finger?" Bishon asked concerned.

"Stupid paper cut, that's all." Jonetta shrugged.

"I called Norman earlier today to ask if it would be alright if I could stop by," Bishon explained his presence. "I guess he never mentioned it to you."

Jonetta shook her head. "I took a nap. Well, I at least tried. He probably didn't want to disturb me."

"I apologize for being angry with you the last time I was here. I wanted to say that to you in person, not over the phone."

Jonetta patted his hand. "I appreciate that."

There was laughter coming from the hallway. Jonetta looked at Bishon, raising her brows. *Who the hell is that?*

"Oh, that's my dad. He wanted to tag along when he found out my plans to stop by today," he smiled sheepishly. "I hope you don't mind."

Jonetta cleared her throat, "Is Barbara here, too?" She refused to refer to her as his "mother".

"No. It's just the fellas. We brought IPA beers and Italian Fiesta pizza as a peace offering."

"Italian Fiesta pizza? Wow! I haven't eaten that since the girls were teenagers. Oldie, but goodie," Jonetta flashed a smile. "I'll be out there in a minute to join you fellas."

"You may need to change that bandage," Bishon said, noticing blood seeping through the tissue.

Jonetta winced at the sight of her own blood, then the pain resonated sending a sharp tingle through her hand. "You'd think I sliced my finger on a knife the way I'm bleeding."

"Is it a really deep paper cut?"

"Deep enough to bleed all over these documents." Jonetta pointed to the nightstand.

"What's all of these envelopes?" Bishon asked, picking up the stack.

"Well, I bled all over Georgia's will. But those are letters I found in her belongings at the house. Colette and I were sorting through her things, getting organized, you know. These stack of envelopes are letters from my mother to me that my sister never gave to me."

"Really?"

"Welcome to the family, son," Jonetta remarked with a chuckle, shaking her head. "So many secrets."

It took her half an hour just to change clothes and decide on shoes. Not that she needed to impress anybody, but she at least wanted to be decent and presentable. She finally settled on an electric blue, silk muumuu that Dawn had bought her in France while at a runway show. Jonetta loved the way it felt, loose and soft, and she paired it with red mules. She intended on looking as good as she could so it can be reported that way to Barbara. Jonetta was ill, but not dead. With a dash of Niki de Saint Phalle perfume behind her ears, she was ready to make an appearance.

When Jonetta emerged from her bedroom, she heard voices coming from the patio. In the kitchen opened the lid on the box of pizza to see what kind it was and decided against eating any. It was sausage. *That's all I need is heartburn all night long.* She frowned at the Anti-Hero IPA beers in the refrigerator. *Clearly they were only thinking of themselves. Where's the wine?* Jonetta exhaled sharply, smoothed her edges, pinched her cheeks and opened the patio door.

"Netta! Glad you could join us," Norman said. He laughed heartily for no apparent reason.

Jonetta eyed the table and counted six empty cans. *One more drink and he'll be drunk.* "Hello, Stanton."

"Join us," Stanton said, pulling out a patio chair.

Jonetta sat quietly as the men engaged in meaningless conversation. They went from sports to traveling to see the Seven Wonders of the World. Neither topic truly interested her as much as calculating her next move with her life. She had serious decisions to make at such a late stage in life.

She watched carefully as Stanton stuffed his face with the greasy pizza and secretly hoped he would choke on it. If Barbara were sitting there devouring the pizza, she'd wish the same fatal disaster on her, too. The only people standing in her way of truly bonding with her only son were Barbara and Stanton. They had to go! She seethed with resentment, eyeing her garden. Norman had been taking good care of it by watering it regularly, but he probably still didn't know about her baneberries hidden behind her herb garden. *Maybe I'll make a batch of special baneberry tea for Barbara and Stanton.*

"Netta?" Norman said.

"Yes?" she was snapped from her wicked thoughts.

"Well? What are you going to do about *your* land?" Norman probed.

"Oh, I just found out about it a few hours ago, Norman. I haven't had the time to process anything," she replied. "I just hope it's worth a chunk of change because I have all of these medical bills flying my way."

"I pulled up the property on Google Maps for you," Bishon said, showing his phone to Jonetta.

"How do you know exactly where it is?" Jonetta asked.

"Norman told us he saw the will, too and the address was listed," Bishon explained.

Jonetta shot Norman a quizzical look. "So now you have a photographic memory in your old age, huh?"

Norman shrugged, opened another can of beer and began gulping it down to avoid confrontation.

"Here," Bishon handed her his phone. "You see it there."

Jonetta squinted, "I can't see much. Just looks like a bunch of dirt."

"There's nothing much to see but land…which is not a bad thing at all. That means more space to build whatever you want on it or you can sell it. I can do more research to see what happened to the house and how many acres you own," Bishon replied, smiling.

"You're always so helpful, Bishon." Jonetta returned the smile and patted his hand. "Honestly, I don't care what happened to the house. I hope it burned to the ground."

All three men stared at her dumbfounded.

"Why?" Bishon asked confused. He looked to Norman for a clue. He had none.

"Just find out about the acres," Jonetta said, nodding. "Thanks."

Bishon cleared his throat, "Well, I've always wanted to know where I come from and it looks like I'm about to find out."

Chapter 29

Ever since Facebook had shut her page down, she had been in a funk. Usually, her days began with reassuring rituals after the girls left for school. *Clean up their bathroom, sweep the stairs, empty the dishwasher, and clean the kitchen thoroughly for the live-stream cooking show.* "Cleanliness is next to Godliness." She could hear her mother say. Even though Jonetta was far from religious, Phyllis figured that she must've gotten that saying from her mother or great aunts. Nevertheless, keeping a well-organized home always helped Phyllis feel balanced and at peace. But ever since she was thrown into Facebook jail, the house chores were neglected.

She had planned on getting back into the swing of things starting today until her phone rang. Just as she was thumbing through her playlist to find the right music for cleaning, Colette's face and number popped up on the screen.

"Good morning, sis. What's up?" Phyllis answered as cheerfully as she could. *It's too early in the morning for drama. Please don't let it be drama.*

"Hey, something has been on my mind that Mama said to me," Colette began, her tone somber.

"Well? What did she say?" Phyllis asked anxiously.

"She said I'm always setting myself on fire to keep other people warm. I had to think about that and…it's true. I'm always putting other people first and neglecting myself."

"We all do to a certain extent, right? Especially women. It's how we keep the family afloat and the household running smoothly as possible. Not to say it's fair, because it's not. I'm just saying, you're not alone and I don't think Mama meant to hurt you by saying that."

"I need a break," Colette admitted. Her tone indicated that she was also in a funk, and that's what concerned Phyllis the most. Colette, a few months ago, had purposely tripped down a flight of stairs in order to miscarry and it worked. Phyllis often wondered if she would go to those extremes over an unwanted pregnancy, what else is she capable of when times are really tough?

"If this is what's on your mind at eight fifty-five in the morning, then yes, I'd have to agree with you," Phyllis chuckled. "But before we plan a getaway, why don't we have a girls' night *out*?"

Colette let out a sigh, "I suppose that should be fine. Is Damien going to watch all the kids?"

Phyllis let out a sharp howl. "Girl, that'll be the day! But I'll certainly ask because Mama and Dad aren't in any shape to handle the twins and your tribe."

"Well, I'm crossing my fingers because I really need a break."

The gurgling noises she heard in the background meant that Delilah was either nursing or burping. "How's Aunty's baby doing?"

"She's fine and getting really fat. I think I'm going to wean her off breastfeeding soon."

"Really? But you nursed your other kids until they were damn near five-years-old!"

Colette laughed. "That's only because Owen was nursing on me, too. He kept my milk flowing more than the kids did all of those years."

"Wait a damn minute! Say what?" Phyllis let out a laugh of disbelief. "Are you serious right now?"

"Yep. I was his favorite snack," Colette confessed nonchalantly.

Phyllis covered her mouth. "Sis, what type of sick-ass-shit is that?"

"Owen's fetish was breast milk," Colette replied. "I'm sure he's over there chugging away on Shante as we speak."

What type of hellish misery has she been putting up with all of these years? Phyllis was completely disgusted and shocked that her sister would allow a man to control her body in such a way. Phyllis didn't entertain that topic anymore. Instead, she began naming locations of where they should go later on.

By the end of their call, Phyllis had organized a girls' night out with her sisters. She had been wanting to discuss in full detail what was happening with the false accusation of child abuse on her Facebook live feed. A change of scenery and fresh air would do them all good.

Dawn had suggested that they do a bar crawl downtown to keep it exciting. The first stop was the VU rooftop in the south loop. She had been wanting to check it out since she had returned home and now was the perfect opportunity. It didn't disappoint. The gas fire pits were lit, although it was a smoldering 83 degrees, it gave the rooftop a swanky appeal. The music was pumping though the surround sound speakers and people were chatting and swaying to the music while waiting in line to order an overpriced drink. It was exactly what summer was about in Chicago.

Phyllis had found a corner for the three of them to sit comfortably.

"I have my eye on that swing," Colette confessed. "As soon as it's free, it's my turn."

They all laughed.

"It's definitely cute," Dawn admitted. "I'll stand in line to get our drinks. Are we sticking with wine or cocktails?"

Phyllis swallowed hard. *I want some vodka so damn bad!* She had promised Damien that she would only drink wine on occasion and was disgruntled about that arrangement. But after she had discovered Port wine with an alcohol content of 20% it was a win-win compromise.

"I'll take a glass of Port wine, if they have it. If not, then a Cabernet will do." Phyllis shrugged.

"I'll take a sparkling water," Colette replied, nodding as if she had just given her final answer on *Ellen's Game of Games.*

"Alrighty then. I'll be back," Dawn said and disappeared into the crowd.

"Well, how do you like this rooftop?" Phyllis asked, bobbing her head to the music. "It's really chic, huh?"

"I'm just happy to be out of the house," Colette said, searching the crowd for Dawn. "It's getting packed up here. I wonder what the capacity limit is on rooftops?" After she experienced a fire in her apartment, looking for an escape route in crowded places had since been part of her thought process.

Phyllis sighed. "Well, that's the furthest thing from my mind. I'm sure we'll be okay. Stop being so paranoid," Phyllis swatted at her knee. "I'm more concerned about these *false* accusations about child abuse taking place in my home."

"What happened?"

"I'll wait until Dawn comes back to fill you in," Phyllis said, patting her sister's knee.

"Oh, here she comes now," Colette perked up, reached for her drink, anxious to quench her thirst. "Thanks, sis." She hurriedly gulped down the clear, ice cold liquid and began to cough.

Dawn snickered, "Are you okay?"

"What the hell is this?" Colette demanded, holding up her cup.

"Vodka tonic with lime," Dawn replied nonchalantly.

Phyllis exchanged glances with Colette and burst into laughter. Dawn began laughing, too, but Colette kept a straight face.

"It's girls' night out. We're *all* drinking. End of story," Dawn explained with a flick of her wrist.

"Cheers," Phyllis held up her drink and took a long gulp of the red wine. She was immediately disappointed when she realized that it wasn't Port wine, but didn't complain. It was alcohol. It was needed.

"Does anyone object to us going inside to sit at a table? I'm burning up like an ant under a microscope!" Colette complained.

"It's just the alcohol racing through you," Phyllis explained. "It'll pass."

Dawn rolled her eyes and snarled. "I guess that I'll have to come back here with folks who know how to hang without complaining."

"Let's go inside for now," Phyllis suggested.

When they headed inside, the cool air that greeted them was immediately a sweet relief. Dawn walked swiftly to a table that was free and sat down, waving her sisters over.

"Hurry up!" Dawn shouted.

"We're coming!" Phyllis shouted back.

Once they were seated comfortably they ordered another round of drinks. Colette insisted that she have sparkling water with olives. She did not like the way alcohol made her feel off balance and out of control. She could experience that all by herself with the help of alcohol.

Phyllis filled them in regarding her Facebook account being deactivated and the reason behind it.

"Well, has DCFS showed up at your door, yet?" Colette asked.

Phyllis shook her head. "No, thank God."

"Then I wouldn't worry about it," Colette advised. "Trust me, when they get involved your whole life will be examined."

"How do you know that?" Dawn asked, sipping her cocktail.

"Oh, please!" Colette rolled her eyes. "You know who I was married to… well…I should say… that man I lived with all these years. The hospital was involved several times and they have the obligation to report any and everything. They wanted to make sure he was not beating on the kids, too."

"Well, did he hit the kids, too?" Phyllis asked, leaning in.

"Hell, no!" Colette answered with a frown on her face. "What type of mother do you think I am?"

Dawn cleared her throat. She signaled for the waitress so she could place another order, this time with another vodka tonic for Colette so she could calm the hell down.

"Phyllis, just open another account under another name," Dawn suggested. "People do that all the time when they're locked up in Facebook jail."

"Or just get on YouTube, create a cooking show page and record to your heart's delight. It's pretty much the same thing. You'll probably get more viewers, too." Colette may not have been good at choosing men, but she was certainly good at getting out of a jam or two.

"That's true," Dawn agreed, stirring her cocktail with a skinny red straw.

"I think I'm just gonna lay-low right now. Damien doesn't want me on social media at all after this fiasco," Phyllis admitted disheartened.

"That's so unrealistic," Dawn remarked, sipping her watered down cocktail and rolling her eyes.

"Is it?" Colette countered. "I rarely get on social media and I'm doing just fine."

"You and senior citizens are just about the only ones who don't engage on social media as a daily routine."

"Maybe you need to detox!" Colette hissed at Dawn.

"Whatever!" Dawn reached for her glass, took a long swallow and emptied her glass.

"Well, Damien wants us to start going back to church and cleansing our spirits of all distractions and pitfalls," Phyllis said, frowning.

"What is that supposed to mean?" Dawn asked. "Y'all got demons or something?"

"Everyone does," Colette remarked. She turned towards Phyllis and squeezed her hand. "Whatever works for you and your family… do it! I just may go to church with you."

The waitress brought their drinks, placed them in a circle of three on the table and bounced away to take more orders.

Perfect timing to change the subject. Dawn had something on her mind that she knew was worth sharing, but didn't know how to quite begin the conversation.

An awkward silence passed between them. Phyllis eyed her new glass of wine and glanced at her half empty wine glass in front of her. *I really shouldn't drink another glass.* She was already feeling lightheaded from the first glass of wine. But the rush felt so good every time she took a sip.

"I went to see him," Dawn blurted out of nowhere.

"Who?" Colette asked, reaching for her water. She took a sip and gave Dawn the evil eye. "This isn't water!"

"Bishon." Dawn ignored Colette and kept the conversation moving. "Our half-brother."

"Why?" Phyllis shrieked.

"Yeah, why?" Colette repeated, sipping slowly on her drink.

"I needed to…I just…" Dawn looked away. She regretted even starting this conversation, but it was too late now. "I needed to know if anything was still there between us so I would know which way to move in my life."

"And?" Phyllis probed, taking a sip of wine.

"And… there is still attraction between us," Dawn admitted.

"What did you do, Dawn?" Colette asked, sucking in her breath.

"Nothing!" she lied.

"So…what are you trying to tell us?" Phyllis demanded impatiently.

"I need to leave this town sooner than later… because I wanted to fuck him all night long!" Dawn admitted, hanging her head in shame.

Colette's mouth flew open as she placed her glass down on the table.

Phyllis threw her hands up in the air. "No! You just returned home to Chicago and now you want to leave again? The better solution would be Bishon taking a back seat and laying low in *all* of our lives. He needs to leave town!"

Colette shrugged. "I don't know, Phyllis. Maybe it's for the best if there's temptation there. Lord knows that we make terrible decisions when we're tempted."

"Oh, really?" Phyllis raised her perfectly arched eyebrows. "Sounds like you're speaking from experience. Care to share?"

"Well, since we're confessing..." Colette began, clearing her throat. "Don't judge me, but Owen came over one night to apologize. We were supposed to talk about coming to an agreement on visitation to present to the courts, you know? But it led to him touching me and I loved feeling his hands all over me. I miss being touched by a man. So, I let him...have his...fetish."

"You let him suck your titties for breast milk?" Phyllis blurted.

"What!?" Dawn shrieked, bucking her eyes.

"Shhhhhh! Would you lower your voices!?" Colette looked around. "He said that mine tastes better than hers."

"What the fuck did I just miss?" Dawn asked, glancing back and forth between her sisters.

Phyllis couldn't do anything but laugh. "Somebody give this girl another round of whatever she's drinking!" Phyllis doubled over laughing at the visual of big-bad Owen latching onto Colette's tit like a little baby. "Girl, this asshole, Owen, has a breast milk fetish."

"Is that why you were never done breastfeeding your kids?" Dawn asked.

"He was my husband. I let him have his way. Big deal," Colette said, taking a sip of Phyllis's wine.

"Hey, don't mix your drinks. You'll be so messed up," Phyllis warned Colette. "How did you not know that you were not married all these years?"

"Dad asked me the same thing," Colette began. "I thought he took care of all the paperwork. I signed everything and he was supposed to file for our marriage license. Honestly, I don't know. It was so long ago."

"And now that you know he's *not* your husband, don't let him fuck you or touch you ever again!" Dawn hissed.

"Yeah, right," Phyllis scoffed and shot a look at Dawn. "Girl, Owen is the only man she's ever been with. It'll happen again and again until she gets tired of playing second fiddle."

"Well, we gotta find you some new dick!" Dawn blurted loud enough for patrons to look in their direction.

Colette was beyond embarrassed. She swatted at Dawn, telling her again to lower her voice when a handsome man approached their table.

"Judge Jamison!" Colette said in a high-pitched tone. *I hope he didn't just hear that!*

Dawn and Phyllis exchanged glances.

"Ms. Miller," he acknowledged.

Colette was impressed that he remembered her name. "I almost didn't recognize you out of your honorable robe."

The sisters collectively eyed his appearance. He was dressed casually in denim jeans, a green Polo shirt and loafers. Whatever cologne he wore was soft yet inviting.

"Are you the judge presiding over her case against that lunatic who's demanding full custody?" Phyllis asked.

"I know you're not going to grant any type of custody to that dirt bag, are you?" Dawn chimed in.

"We can't ask him that! Please don't go ruining my case!" Colette snapped at her sisters.

The judge laughed off their questions. "Ladies, I'm not at liberty to comment."

"I'm so sorry about that. Please excuse my sisters." Colette flushed with embarrassment and shot daggers towards Phyllis and Dawn.

"No worries," he chuckled. "Nothing wrong with a great supportive family." Colette was right, he couldn't answer those questions, but he did want to share a few thoughts with her. The judge swirled his brown liquor in his glass before he began. "Ms. Miller, I hear many cases presented before me, but yours in particular has been heavy on my mind. I was nine-years-old when my mother committed suicide a few months after giving birth to my sister. She was only thirty-four years old, suffering from post-partum depression. Back then, they called it the 'Baby Blues'."

"Oh, my God! I'm so sorry to hear that," Colette replied, covering her mouth. Although she definitely felt empathy for his life, she cringed just the same, hoping that his next words wouldn't reveal her business like Owen did in court because her sisters were none the wiser. *Please don't mention anything about my suicide attempt.*

He nodded. "That does something to a kid. Life is never the same without your mother. We only get one," he lamented. "I'm grateful that I actually have memories of my mother, but my sister never knew her… and it shows."

Colette quietly exhaled.

"That's so terrible," Phyllis said. "I can't imagine life without our mother. I'm sorry for your loss."

"Thank you. But I shared that with you to say, I'm not in favor of splitting up families whether they be illegal immigrants, grandparents seeking full custody, or husbands using the children to spite the wife or vice versa. Ms. Miller, even when things seem like they are not going in your favor, be strong and have faith that everything will work out the way it should. If you need help, don't be afraid to ask. We have a lot more resources these days than we did back in the sixties, thank God."

"Thank you," Colette replied with her bottom lip quivering. Judge Jamison took a long gulp of his liquor and placed the empty glass on their table. "Have a good evening, ladies."

"He's not going to grant that asshole custody of your kids, sis," Dawn said, squeezing Colette's hand.

"Definitely not," Phyllis agreed. "I think he just said it *without* saying it."

"And he's looking like a whole snack! He remembered your whole name, too! Looks like new dick to me!" Dawn howled, giving Phyllis a high-five.

With tears in her eyes, Colette watched him saunter out the door. As much as she wanted to bite back her stinging tears, they instead escaped freely down her cheeks.

Chapter 30

She had received the text message later in the morning. With sleep in her eyes, she barely made out the message. Her mother wanted to see her face and needed her help prepping for their family Labor Day barbeque. Dawn tried to recall the last time that she had cooked in anybody's kitchen. *It must've been last Thanksgiving that I helped cook anything. I am not the one!* She placed the phone underneath her pillow and moaned.

Dawn didn't want to cook or be in the kitchen at all, instead, the little girl in her wanted to curl up in her mother's lap and sob until her soul was cleansed. There was so much on her mind as of late. Constantly worrying about her future, next move, dividing the family and most importantly, her mother's love. Was it truly unconditional? Or did she have the privilege of choosing which child to love?

For as long as she could remember, she had been her mother's favorite. Dawn was the baby, cute, honey brown complexion, curly hair, full of energy and life. She brought sunshine to the day and life to the party. Her sisters knew she was the favorite, too. Phyllis being the oldest daughter felt responsible for her baby sister, so she rarely had envious moments. Colette on the other hand used to hide toys, shoes, and anything she could think of from Dawn. Jonetta always dressed up Dawn like a doll baby. Colette grew resentful because she just didn't think it was fair to dote over one daughter. Why not all of them?

For the most part, everybody babied her, up until her late teens. Around that time Phyllis had a life of her own as Damien's wife and Colette was on baby number two with Owen. Nobody had time to spoil her anymore. That's when she turned to smoking weed and drinking. Moving to New York to model only fed into her drug habits. She was the "It Girl" on the rise. The little girl in her didn't have a voice anymore. She grew up and made some really bad decisions. The bed she made was rock hard. Her cries went unnoticed.

Dawn swung her feet around, placed them on the floor and stretched her arms to the sky as far as they could go. When she finally exhaled, she listened for the regular morning ritual noises, but there were none. She picked up her phone to check the time. *It's no wonder why it's so quiet. It's Sunday.* Phyllis had mentioned that her family would be attending Friends and Family Day at Damien's former church. He thought it was time for them to rededicate their lives to the Lord.

Dawn had told Phyllis that she was on her own and not to even think about inviting her to church. She walked to her top dresser drawer, grabbed a stick of white sage and burned it with her lighter. She grabbed her yoga mat from the closet, rolled it out and began stretching.

Yoga was introduced to her in New York by another model who seemed always so balanced and calm in the midst of chaos. Ever since Dawn went to a yoga class with her, it had become part of her life. But when she moved back to Chicago, she rarely had the opportunity. She sat Indian style on the mat, closed her eyes and practiced breathing techniques. She wanted to be prepared for whatever came her way today.

***

"You're always running, girl." Jonetta shook her head, stirring a large boiling pot of macaroni noodles. Jonetta knew that Dawn wasn't the chef in the family, but she could at least help dice potatoes, if nothing else.

"I'm not running, Mama," Dawn refuted. "I'm going to be domesticated. Isn't that what you suggested?"

"I thought you said that Vine was gay?"

Dawn had shared with her mother that she got in contact with Vine and they were discussing reconciling which meant she would relocate to Atlanta. Now she regretted mentioning it at all. "He's not gay. Trannies are very common and apparently everywhere in Atlanta. He didn't know that he was dating a man until… well… you know, it was time to find out."

Jonetta narrowed her suspicious eyes and frowned her face in disgust. She shook her head. "Well, did he do it?"

"What!? Mama, no! He kicked her ass out… or *his* ass out the moment he discovered that they were delivering the same package down there."

"That's a sure fire way to get killed!" Jonetta replied, mashing her cigarette in a tray. "If Vine was another type of man from Chicago, that transvestite would've been beat to death."

Dawn snickered, "That didn't come out right, Mama. But, you're right. Vine wouldn't harm a fly."

Jonetta eyed her youngest daughter carefully. The very mention of Vine's name spread a gleam of joy across her face. "You're really leaving me again, huh?"

"Sometimes a change is needed," Norman said, emerging from the bedroom. "Just don't go down there getting into trouble."

"That's like telling water not to be wet!" Jonetta retorted.

Dawn frowned. "I cannot change my experiences and choices. It is what it is. Sorry to disappoint you, but I am who I am."

"Nobody is asking you to change, so just calm down and stop being so dramatic," Norman shook his head. He pulled a chair closer to Dawn at the kitchen table and took a seat.

"Just make better choices," Jonetta advised with a wink.

"All I'm saying is change is good," Norman continued. "There's nothing wrong with evolving. You probably need a change of pace, a change of scenery. You know… something to get your mind off of things. You've had a tough break kiddo."

Dawn lowered her head in shame. "I couldn't agree more, Dad."

"I know you feel that everyone is rallying around Bishon since your mother has been out of the hospital, but believe me baby girl, it's not a day that goes by that I don't feel for you." Norman lifted his daughter's chin until her big brown eyes met his. "Don't let the unknown of the past haunt and destroy your future. Just let it go, baby. Chin up."

Dawn straightened her posture, lifted her head and nodded.

"Nobody is 'rallying around Bishon'," Jonetta argued. "I'm simply trying to welcome *my* son into this family, but everyone, except Colette is making it extremely difficult."

Dawn nodded, fighting back tears. "I can't even look at him. I'm just too ashamed and disgusted. Mama wants us to be one big happy family. None of you can even imagine what I'm going through."

"Listen, as much as I hate to admit this, because you're my baby girl and all… but, it sounds like you need a change of scenery." Jonetta conceded.

Dawn nodded in agreement at that idea. "Dad, I'm in desperate need for a change. I'm feeling like I need to head to Atlanta to be with Vine. Maybe it's time for me to settle down. I haven't done modeling work in over six months now. I think there's more opportunity down there for me, but I wouldn't even know where to begin."

"Don't worry about all of that," Norman consoled her. "Let's just take one day at a time. You'll find your way."

By the time the potatoes were done boiling, Dawn had taken over making the potato salad with Jonetta's specific instruction. Jonetta had grown weary standing up longer than an hour. She had over extended her energy and Dawn noticed it immediately.

"I'll take over from here, Mama." Dawn had guided her mother to a chair in the kitchen. "Just tell me exactly what to do." Although her body was tired, Jonetta was still of sound mind. A wide grin spread across Dawn's face when the outcome looked and tasted just like Jonetta had made it. She pulled out her iPhone, snapped a picture to post on Instagram.

"Don't get too happy. Hold on a second," Norman said grabbing a spoon from the kitchen drawer. "I have to give the stamp of approval and then you can post your picture."

Dawn giggled while she watched her father dip his spoon in the creamy potato salad and stuff his mouth. The smile that crept across his face was all the approval she needed.

"Now *that's* your Mama's recipe, for sure!" Norman belted out a deep laugh and gave Dawn a thumbs up.

As soon as Dawn opened the Instagram app, the first post she saw was from Vine. It was a cup of coffee with a creamy foam shaped in a heart. The caption underneath the picture read: *Thinking of you…*

Chapter 31

Nobody needed a reminder about today. Even the children were up early in the morning, anxious for their annual Labor Day barbeque. Colette had been rounding up games and sports balls all morning to ensure the kids had enough to do, especially Cornell. He was the oldest of their children and the only boy which meant, usually there were only girlie activities or toys at their family gatherings. Colette was determined this year to at least teach the girls how to play softball so Cornell could participate too. For good measure, she asked Phyllis to order a volleyball net and she'd supply the ball.

Phyllis and Colette had agreed last year during Easter dinner that no technology for the kids would be allowed at family functions. They needed to grow up as cousins who played together, the old-fashioned-way. There was always a board game, UNO, jump rope, or a deck of cards handy. This time there would be a sports game for healthy competition amongst the whole family. Phyllis had also ordered six burlap sacks from Amazon and hid them in the trunk of Damien's SUV. The twins were busy-bodies these days and she didn't want spank or fuss at anybody for touching them. Not today. The adults were going to participate, too, and she couldn't wait to win. This was one of her favorite holidays. It was never too hot or too cold. The weather was usually perfect.

Damien usually did all the grilling, but this year Norman decided to season slabs of ribs and help guard the grill. Although half of the family had sworn off pork, he knew that between Damien, Jonetta and himself they would gobble them up and save whatever they couldn't eat for the rest of the week. There was nothing like some good barbeque ribs with homemade potato salad, according to Norman, and Dawn had put her foot in the potato salad on her first try.

The clouds finally broke around nine o'clock in the morning, allowing the sunshine to brighten their day. Dawn had finished stretching and was headed to the shower when she heard muffled moaning from Phyllis and Damien's bedroom. A tinge of jealousy shot through her as she secretly wished it was her climaxing this morning. *Soon enough I'll be back in Atlanta with Vine.* She closed the bathroom door softly, opened her robe and stared at her breasts in the mirror. She squeezed them gently and smiled. *Good. No more milk.*

Once in the shower, she ran warm water and soaked herself from head to toe. She allowed her thoughts to travel back to making love to Vine as she massaged mint shampoo into her scalp. He was nowhere near as passionate as Bishon, now that she thought about it. In comparison, her love-making with Vine was still stuck at second base compared to the homeruns Bishon made in the bedroom. And she couldn't help but think about Raffi who had years of built up anticipation waiting to explode. It was damn near magical. *And I have to give up all of that good dick? God, this is so unfair!*

She inhaled sharply at the thought of Bishon showing up to their annual family Labor Day barbeque. It had totally slipped her mind to ask her mother if she had invited him. She hurriedly rinsed the shampoo from her hair, lathered it with leave-in mint conditioner and grabbed her towel. Before she could even completely dry off, she picked up her iPhone and almost called her mother until she realized that all she had to do was check Bishon's social media's pages first. If she couldn't find a clue there what his intentions were today, then she'd call her mother.

It appeared that he had not logged on over the past three days, not even on his dental page. The last time they were together, she was so high and emotional that she was positive that she had made some bad decisions. She simply couldn't remember them. All she remembered was his hands caressing every inch of her body and then she woke up next to him, embarrassed.

For whatever reason Dawn couldn't reach Bishon nor Jonetta. The moment she saw Phyllis emerge from her bedroom she asked if she had heard from their mother. She hadn't. Now Dawn was in a foul mood over it.

"I'm sure she's just getting ready for the day at her own pace," Phyllis said. "What's the urgency?"

"I need to know if our half-brother plans on attending," Dawn explained.

"So why not just call him?"

Really? Dawn shook her head no.

"I hope he doesn't come to our family barbeque. Have we even discussed how we would integrate him into family functions?"

Dawn shrugged, "Not officially."

"Then he shouldn't show up today."

Dawn had hoped Phyllis was right about her theory. But she knew her mother even better. *She wants Bishon involved in every little thing we do.*

The moment they pulled up to their designated grove at the Dan Ryan Woods, Dawn immediately regretted not driving her own car. There he was, sitting on the bench chatting it up with Jonetta. Dawn cringed.

"Fuck!" Dawn blurted out.

"Ohhhh! Aunty Dawn said a bad word!" Serena wailed.

"Dawn!" Phyllis hissed from the passenger seat.

"My bad," Dawn apologized, patting her niece's head. "Aunty Dawn has a potty mouth. I'm sorry."

"That's okay. Daddy said that word this morning, too, when he forgot his keys upstairs," Sabrina said, giggling.

They all cracked up laughing and began unloading the trunk. Norman came over to help unload the heavy items.

"Hey, Dad!" Dawn and Phyllis said in unison, smothering him in hugs.

"Nobody told us we were having a guest," Dawn remarked.

"Don't start," Norman warned. "Your mother is in a good mood."

"I've been calling her all morning," Dawn said.

Norman shrugged. "We're all here now. Let's have some fun."

Dawn greeted Jonetta with a kiss on the cheek ignoring Bishon and began to set up the picnic table. *I'm not even gonna say anything. But I am about to pop a gummy bear in two minutes.* Bishon acknowledged the cold shoulder and approached Dawn while she was setting up the table with food and snacks. "Hey, everything is looking good," he chuckled nervously as he tried to make small talk. "Need some help?"

Dawn didn't make eye contact nor make a sound. *Just go away.*

"Listen," Bishon cleared his throat. "I've been thinking about the last time we saw each other. And… that has to be the last time we…"

"We didn't do anything!" Dawn cut him off abruptly. She looked around to see if anyone had noticed her outburst. Thankfully, the rest of the family was busy putting up the volleyball net and Jonetta was fussing at Norman. "I'm moving to Atlanta soon. So you can have my mother all to yourself. Things won't be awkward anymore. Everyone can just move on… in peace. Okay?"

"Oh…" Bishon replied, rubbing the back of his neck.

"When do you leave?"

"I said soon."

"I hope you aren't leaving because of me."

"Don't be so arrogant all the time. Everything isn't about you!" she lied. *Of course, I'm leaving my family because of you. Why else would I leave when I just got here?* Dawn began to quiver at the thought of leaving her mother again. Not seeing her face regularly was going to get the best of her. She loved her mother and sisters. But she had no choice except to leave before she made another mistake, like getting pregnant.

"I really wish you would stay. We can work things out as a family. I mean, look at us," Bishon opened his arms towards the family. "We all belong together so we can know one another better, spend time and…"

"I think you and I have spent way too much time together already. The last thing I need is to wake up in your bed again. I'm ashamed about that and whatever happened," Dawn admitted, arranging the potato salad on a bed of ice. "Do you know how sick to my stomach I feel knowing that you are my brother and that we had sex? Not just sex, but *really* good sex multiple times."

The look of disgust on Dawn's face was enough for Bishon to not press the issue any further. She was moving away and he had to accept that.

"Well, I hope you find what you're looking for in Atlanta," Bishon conceded, placing his hands on her shoulders and kissing her forehead.

Before Dawn could respond, she saw Owen walking towards them. "Colette! What's Owen doing here?"

Colette frowned with confusion, spun around to quickly look over her shoulder to see the devil himself approaching. In a wife-beater, baggy jeans and Nike slide-ons, he flashed a smiled as he got closer. "I have no idea. We haven't worked out any visitation or holiday schedule yet."

"Wassup fam?" Owen greeted them as he strolled across the grass.

The children were too engrossed in playing their second round of kickball to notice their father. Colette was thankful.

"Fam?" Phyllis scoffed.

"What are you doing here? How did you even find us?"

Colette inquired with one hand on her hip.

Owen pulled his phone from his pocket, waving it in her face with a sly grin. “I downloaded a app on the phone I gave Cornell to locate my kids at all times... Duh!”

He embraced Colette with a sensual hug, rubbing his hands up and down her back and she pulled away. Alcohol seeped from him pores.

“Don’t touch me like that!”

“Oh, now I can’t touch you because you in front of your family, huh? That’s cool. I’ll see you Wednesday.”

“You’ve been drinking and you should leave,” Colette said firmly.

“I totally hate him right now,” Phyllis remarked, shaking her head.

“Girl, same!” Dawn replied with a look of disgust across her face.

“The feeling is mutual, sis,” Owen replied to Phyllis, nodding.

“I’m not your damn ‘sis’!” Phyllis countered walking towards him. “You were never married to my sister, remember?”

“Babe,” Damien said, pulling her arm. “Be cool.”

“Phyllis, I got this,” Colette said holding her arm out to keep Phyllis out of Owen’s reach.

“You ain’t got shit, but my kids! It’s the holiday and I wanna spend time with them, too! Now go get ‘em so I can bounce.” Owen demanded sucking on a toothpick.

“I’m not doing shit! You are not driving drunk with *my* kids in the car!” Colette replied fiercely, raising her voice loud enough for the birds to fly away. Her eyes darted quickly to the children. From the looks of things, they hadn’t heard her or noticed their father yet. *Thank God!*

Norman stood and slowly walked towards Owen. He wanted to punch his lights out, but refrained from making a scene in front of the children and Jonetta. Instead, he remained calm, yet firm when he spoke. “Owen, I’m not going to allow you to disrespect my daughter nor anybody in my family! You need to make arrangements to see your children like most men do when they abandon their family. You can’t just pop-up demanding to take them away from their family gathering whenever you feel like it."

"I don't want my children around this type of family!" Owen growled.

"What the hell is that supposed to mean?" Jonetta asked, attempting to stand.

Phyllis patted her on the shoulder and shook her head. "No, Mama. Don't let him get you all riled up. He's not worth your health."

"We don't want you having a setback, Mama. Please don't get worked up," Damien pleaded with Jonetta. He stood behind her just in case she fainted, but was fully prepared to whoop Owen's ass if need be.

"All these years this Miller family has looked down on me, my brothers, and my mother for being fucked up one way or the other! But at least we were out in the open with our shit. We ain't fake and shit like y'all. Yep, we do drugs. Yep, we drank. Yep, we slap women around when they need it. Yep, we're womanizers. Yep, we stay broke. And everybody knows it and still rock with us!" Owen shouted with his arms flailing around. "But y'all? Oh, y'all a special breed. Y'all out here doing incest and shit. Gambling. Prostituting. And…Beating your kids on social media."

"Watch your damn mouth, Owen!" Damien threatened.

"You don't know what the hell you're talking about!"

"Oh, yes, I do!" he laughed wickedly.

"Are you on dope right now, Owen? You've gone too damn far this time!" Norman warned. "You better leave or it just might get ugly!"

"No! I ain't gone far enough yet! Y'all the ones out here ratchet. Ain't that right, Dawn? Still fuckin' your brother, huh?"

"What the hell? You don't know shit!" Dawn snapped, pointing her finger in his direction.

Bishon pulled her by the arm. "Don't feed into his rage."

"It's written all over y'all face! Look at your body language. Yep, your brother still hitting that!"

"You had better shut-the-fuck-up about my life and worry about your own sad excuse for a life!"

"Or what?" Owen opened his arms. "What y'all gonna do? Report me for telling the truth!? Too late because I already reported y'all!"

They all glanced at one another, confused.

"What are you talking about?" Colette asked, folding her arms across her heaving chest.

"Yeah, that was me reporting your funky ass, Phyllis!" Phyllis was in a state of disbelief. "What did you say?"

"You heard me! I. Reported. Your. Funky. Ass. To. Facebook."

Phyllis gasped sharply. "Why would you do that?"

"Because you think you the shit and you not," Owen chuckled. "Somebody had to humble your ass. Damien fa sho don't know how! Just ask you sister how I humbled her ass! I can give you some lessons on how to humble your loud mouth wife, Damien."

Phyllis grabbed a white plastic fork from the table and lunged towards Owen, aiming for his throat. Damien and Norman managed to pull her off of him before she was able to puncture him and before he was able to land a punch. They all knew he wasn't above hitting a woman.

Jonetta marched towards the mayhem with a baseball bat they had brought for the kids, lifted her arm to swing, but Colette had finished the fiasco by slapping him hard across his face forcefully.

"Get your ass in the car and LEAVE! Just get the hell outta here before I call the police!"

Just as Owen raised his hand to strike Colette, Damien came from his left side, struck him in the jaw and knocked him out with one clean punch.

Chapter 32

What should have been a day of family, food and fun had turned out to be a day of unexpected events. After Owen was dragged back to his car by Norman and Damien, thankfully, the children never laid eyes on him. They made sure that when he came to that he was well enough to drive off from the park and he did, quietly.

Everything had seemed to calm down amongst the adults until Bishon wanted a private conversation with Jonetta.

"I found out more about your property in Pennsylvania," Bishon began, sliding next to her on the bench.

"What's the verdict?"

"It's almost an acre of land. The house was demolished about fifteen years ago."

"I wouldn't even call it a house," Jonetta remarked bitterly, rolling her eyes. "It was more like a two-room shack that needed to be demolished long time ago."

"But the land isn't fertile enough to grow crops or anything," Bishon continued. He had decided not to probe her further for information. The last time he did, it didn't go so well.

Jonetta scoffed. "It never was."

"Well, it's all yours. You can keep it or sell it for a small profit."

Jonetta nodded. "I'll have Norman look into selling it. Maybe it'll help pay off some of these medical bills."

"You don't want to go see the land at least?"

"No!" Jonetta replied fiercely. "That's one memory lane I'm not interested in traveling back down."

"Understood," Bishon replied solemnly.

"I appreciate you looking into it for me, though." Jonetta squeezed his hand.

"Also, I wanted to share with you that… Well, I just… I think you should know that I still have feelings for Dawn," he admitted, searching her eyes for understanding.

A look of shock and disgust spread across her face. "Why do you think that I wanted to know that?"

"Listen… I'm not trying to hurt you or anyone," he began to explain nervously. "I'm just being honest and I hate that it has to be this way. I know right from wrong and I certainly know that incest is wrong. This whole family dynamic is awkward and uncomfortable for everyone. Look at them," he nodded in their direction. "They avoid me like the plague. Nobody has come towards us since I sat next to you. It shouldn't be that way. You're their mother, too."

"Don't pay them any mind, son. This is all new to everyone. They'll come around," Jonetta tried to smooth things over.

"That's hardly the point," Bishon exhaled sharply. "Ever since I found out that you were my birth mother it has caused friction in this family. Mine included. My mother has been suffering from anxiety about who I'm going to choose as a mother!

She acts like I'm a six-year-old who needs to tell a judge which family I want to live with from now on. All of that stress on her is just so unnecessary."

"Well, it's not like they legally adopted you," Jonetta remarked.

Bishon shook his head. "My point is, none of that even matters. They raised me. They are my parents."

Jonetta looked hurt by his truth and sat quiet for a moment. "I was robbed of my opportunity to raise you as my child. I was lied to about your existence. I thought you were dead for over forty years. Imagine how I feel."

Bishon exhaled, wrapped his arm around her shoulder and whispered, "I can't imagine and I'm so sorry that happened to you."

Never one for making a public scene, Jonetta held back tears. "Nobody understands."

"I know that's why Dawn is moving to Atlanta… to get far away from me. But, please know that I'm not trying to divide this family. I just wanted to be part of it. Part of your life, finally. But I think it's probably best that I give it more time and give everyone a lot more space."

"So, I'm losing my only son and youngest daughter all in one week?" Jonetta said with disbelief and sadness.

"I'm so sorry. I have to go." Bishon had left the park with apologies and excuses. If he had a tail, it'd be so far tucked between his legs it would've looked like a penis.

By the time Jonetta laid her head to rest that evening, she reflected on how life had taken a turn of events. Despite how she felt about Dawn moving to Atlanta, she understood exactly why she was determined even more so now that Bishon had expressed his feelings. Jonetta couldn't see it before, but Dawn wasn't running away, she was running towards a new life. It was best.

A smile crept across her face when Colette flashed before her eyes. She had finally stood up for herself. She faced the biggest demon in her life, Owen, and survived unscathed. Jonetta's heart swelled with pride. *That's my girl!* Jonetta could only hope that he would get the message loud and clear now. Owen had finally been put in his place. It was the highlight of her day.

Once Bishon left the premises, Phyllis moved in quickly to update her mother on her news. She was vamping up her YouTube page for recipes and would feature gardening tips by Colette. "One monkey don't stop no show!" Phyllis claimed. Her spirits were lifted again, especially because Damien actually supported this mission.

Before she could replay the full day, she had drifted off to a well-deserved sleep. Georgia appeared extending her hand towards her. She was glowing a golden hue, inviting and tempting to follow. Jonetta was happy to see her sister's face so vivid and warm.

I'm so sorry, Georgia. It was an accident. I was trying to poison Big Louie, not you.

I know. I forgive you.

Why didn't you give me the letters from Mama all these years?

Will you forgive me, Netta?

I have no choice, Georgia.

You gave me the gift of a second chance to be with my Gabe. He is here with me. Look who else is here.

Jonetta turned in slow motion to see Mr. Lucky. She could've sworn that she smelled his cologne, Brut by Faberge, just as clear as day. He was dressed in all white, extending his hand, flashing that winning smile.

Come be with us, Johnnie.

She hated that nickname so much that she flinched in her sleep and it shook her woke. "No. My family needs me."

The End

About The Author

Rebekah S. Cole is a fresh literary pearl from Chicago, IL. In March 2016, her debut novel, Women's Voices was published and received rave reviews. Thanks to the feedback from readers she decided to create a sequel, Jonetta's Death. Rebekah continues to write realistic, fluid novels that showcases relatable characters with human issues. Follow her on social media for more updates.

Rebekah S. Cole

Email: beckywrites2@gmail.com

Facebook: www.facebook.com/rebekahscole

Instagram: www.instagram.com/rebekahscole

Twitter: @rebekahScole

Synopsis

JONETTA, matriarch of the Miller family, put most of her secrets on the table. A fresh start was hers for the taking, but she soon learns that she wasn't the only one harboring secrets all these years. New discoveries from her past changes everything.

PHYLLIS finds purpose as a housewife by streaming her own cooking show live, but things go awry with her husband Damien when she allows her suspicions of his infidelity to get the best of her.

DAWN enjoys her freedom but her best friend, Chena, has a dying wish that will test their friendship and sanity as Dawn tries to balance a new relationship with Dr. Bishon Franklyn and two households.

COLETTE finds life after Owen by working at her church as the new secretary. She has her sights set on the pastor not realizing his past and connection to her mother.

This time revenge and secrecy have gone too far as The Miller Family returns in this sequel to ***Women's Voices***. For a family bound together by deceit, their truths will come at a devastating price.

Made in the USA
Monee, IL
19 August 2023

41268258R00121